THE FURTHER TRAVELS

AND

SURPRISING ADVENTURES

OF BARON MUNCHAUSEN

ALSO BY ROSS STEIN

Diary of a Heretic

The Further Travels and Surprising Adventures of Baron Munchausen

Gray Area Press

Publisher, Copyright, and Additional Information

The Further Travels and Surprising Adventures of Baron Munchausen
by Ross Stein published by Gray Area Press

ISBN 979-8-9857162-5-2

rosssteinbooks.com

Illustrations by Charles Delaune

Cover design by Luisa Galstyan

It should come as no surprise to the casual reader that the event that I am about to relate, and coincidentally all subsequent events as they were related to me, will seem to be of an incomparably extraordinary nature; indeed, this very same nature would situate said events among the highest, most esteemed position of all those stories enshrined in the pantheon of what, in the common parlance, is referred to as the—and permit me to add here the somewhat vertically inaccurate—tall tale.

Nevertheless, the story committed to the confines of these pages remains the whole, absolute, and undeniable truth. I leave it to the good sense of my capable reader to weigh for himself the veracity of this most amazing account.

Most humbly yours,

The Author

It transpired one particular afternoon after I'd completed my daily quota of pages that I found myself sitting alone at a corner table near the back of the Mare's End, enjoying a well-earned and well-deserved libation. I'd arrived early for our appointment, as was my habit, and to calm my nerves a bit, I'd brought along an old, weather-beaten copy of *Tristram Shandy* to help pass the time. I was well into my second bottle of beer when the decidedly peculiar figure of my long-anticipated companion caught my eye as he entered the bar.

I recognized him immediately, though, to tell the truth, I wasn't entirely sure I'd seen him at all at first. However, this was not an occurrence so out of the ordinary. Such is the ethereal nature of the baron. At once both real and imaginary, his has always been a personage that bridged the cosmic gap of both space and time. Much as the mighty legs of the fabled Colossus straddled the harbor at Rhodes, so, too, did the baron stand bestride the tangible and the illusory—always with one foot firmly planted on the ground, even as the other tiptoed on a cloud.

I'd not seen him in years, but the intervening seasons had not much changed him. A little whiter at the temples, a little less sure in his stride, perhaps, but nonetheless unmistakably the baron.

His name had been dancing on the lips of the public for months as unbelievable stories of his travels across America spread over the airwaves. Bold-faced headlines two inches high splashed front pages from New York to San Francisco: "Munchausen Swims Up Niagara Falls!" and "Munchausen Takes Checkered Flag at Daytona in Homemade Pedal Car!" Almost nightly, the evening news had run at least one piece, usually two minutes of fluff, to round out the broadcast, detailing how he'd been spotted ascending Mount Hood alone with nothing but a derby-handle walking cane and a three-foot length of nylon rope, or that he'd emerged from the Appalachian foothills near Johnson City, Tennessee, carrying thirty freshly slain black bears slung over his shoulders and wearing an eastern box turtle shell the size of a Galapagos tortoise on his head like an M1917 helmet.

From Reno, they said an incredible streak of luck broke the banks at both the Peppermill and the El Dorado casinos. Twenty-seven consecutive full houses capped off by an impossible royal flush with not one but two queens of hearts! In Atlanta, at the Georgia Aquarium, he was said to have spent almost four hours retrieving his hat from the belly of Trixie, the whale shark, when the old girl swallowed it. Witnesses reported it had inopportunely slipped off his head while he was enjoying a leisurely ride on the back of a manta ray.

They said he traveled almost exclusively on foot, and only rarely by car or rail, and that flying in the cramped cabin of a modern jet airplane offended his constitution and sense of privacy. Corporate interests, from Apple to Amazon to Walmart, offered him the unlimited use of their more accommodating, more luxurious, and certainly more expedient executive air services, all clamoring over each other, salivating at the opportunity to attach a name of such renown to their entities. The baron politely refused all offers with a wink and a smile, noting there wasn't anywhere he could not get to with only his own two legs to carry him, if not occasionally helped along by the fortuitous appearance of a passing seahorse or giant eagle.

I'd heard a state parade in his honor was at that very moment scheduled to commence in Washington, DC. Emissaries and representatives from more than forty nations had flown in to attend. Twelve West African lions were harnessed three abreast to draw the baron's gold-plated phaeton down Pennsylvania Avenue. Fashioned from the carapace of an enormous horseshoe crab draped in laurel wreaths and flowing silk banners six hundred feet long, the carriage itself would be trailed by three separate marching bands comprised entirely of trained lowland gorillas. Hawaiian fire dancers and a cavalcade of Bedouin princes on camelback would lead the procession. The event was to be broadcast live across the globe. Even the SETI Institute got in on the game, arranging for a radio transmission of the festivities to be beamed directly toward the exoplanet Gliese 667 Cc in the Scorpius constellation in the hopes that if there is anyone there, they might be as excited to learn of the baron's exploits as the people of Earth. At the end of the parade route, he was to give a speech on the steps of the Capitol, and one could only believe his message would be one of peace and praise for what the great land of America had blossomed into from its humble, arduous beginnings.

But there would be no speech, and the phaeton would roll empty down the grand avenue, for when the time came to start the parade, the baron was nowhere to be found. I was honored he'd elected to forgo the festivities in favor of meeting with me instead.

"An ale, my good man. And don't be stingy with the foam."

The bartender of the Mare's End switched the television over to the live coverage of the parade, then mechanically grabbed the tap and poured a golden brew for his newest patron. He took no notice whatsoever of the baron's personage, or if he did, he appeared unmoved. It's in the nature of bartenders to listen to sob stories and the occasional outlandish tale but to care little from whose mouth they spill, be he a boozer, a broken heart, or a baron.

Munchausen graciously accepted the proffered glass, lifting the sweaty pint to his lips. Drinking half the lot in one go, the bulging

apple in his throat made considerable leaps up and down his neck as the cool ale washed down his gullet. With one final gulp, the remainder was gone. He smacked his lips and called for another.

"And, this time, I shall use a vessel of my own choosing," he said, his voice creaky as an old wooden door. "If you would permit me, my good man?" The barkeep, not quite sure what to make of it, stepped aside while the baron coolly strode around the back of the bar and from within the folds of his crimson hussar's coat produced a crystal stein of immense proportion, as tall as a man plus three feet, with a circumference of nearly the same measure. A pewter escutcheon bearing the royal coat of arms of the king of Brobdingnag gave reference to its illustrious origins.

"A gift from an old traveling companion," the baron clucked as he topped off his beer. The bartender could only watch gape-mouthed as the last drops of his stock poured out into the near-bottomless well of the glass. But Munchausen, no skinflint, left a brick of hundred-dollar bills on the bar for his tab.

"You should find this more than adequately compensates you, my good sir. And as for the rest, a bottle of your finest red and perhaps a plate of kippers?"

By now, the parade on the television had started. Wolf Blitzer, joined by Lester Holt, Mika Brzezinski, Chris Wallace, Anderson Cooper, Jeanine Pirro, and Laura Ingraham provided running commentary. The Great Sphinx of Giza, having been restored to its original splendor and gratefully donated by the government of Egypt for the occasion, glided past the camera, pushed by Pantagruel, the giant king of the Dipsodes, while his father, Gargantua, trailed behind bearing the *Statue of Unity* (on loan from India) on his shoulders, all to the cheers and horror of the spectators lining the avenue.

The baron finished his mug of beer, drinking it off in long, heaving draughts, down to the last bubbles of creamy white foam, and spilled not a single drop of the precious liquid. Then he took up a glass and the bottle of Malbec left by the barkeep and eased himself into a seat opposite my own to await his plate of kippers.

The leather chair accepted its honored guest with an agreeable sigh and welcomed him like a warm embrace, even as the other denizens of the bar regarded his outlandish presence with almost alien bewilderment. The baron always was a peacock among pigeons, but like a good soldier, he maintained a militant aplomb amid the gawkers.

Regarding his carriage, it can be said he bore himself upright with soldierly pride, or at least as much uprightness as his old bones would allow. The passing years had lent his shoulders a modest slump, his spine the gentlest—one might even call it graceful—curvature, like that of a bulrush giving ever so slightly to a passing autumn breeze. A regal curve really detracting not a whit from his elegant mien, but enhancing it, even, somehow lending more gravity to his poise. He carried this frame on long, sturdy legs, strong and lean as a bull's, so that, despite the bend, he still towered nearly a head taller than most other men in the room. And when he sat, he crossed those sinewy legs with all the intent of a man setting the jaws of a steel bear trap.

His nose was exceedingly long, with two serious brown eyes set narrowly on either side of its cuspate bridge. His face, like his legs, was lean, and his cheeks drew marginally inward, giving his jaw a sturdy, angular line that tapered severely down to a pointed chin that jutted forward like a knife, at the tip of which grew a snowy tuft of hair lovingly teased and waxed into a sharp Vandyke. A pair of thin, bloodless lips concealed a mouthful of well-kept porcelain dentures only moderately yellowed from his near-constant use of tobacco. Above these grew a pencil-thin mustache, white as his beard, curled into upturned points. Tucked between these lips, he kept an old briarwood pipe from which he puffed occasionally, screwing up his eyes into pensive slits, giving over to his whole visage the look of a man deep in intense thought and measure.

Ever the man of action, his uniform bore the memories of bloody battles fought on far-off Ottoman fields of war, his boots trailing the dust of Crimea, Gibraltar, Ceylon, and countless other exotic lands in his wake. His white breeches showed wear at the seams from years in the saddle, but gold braided epaulettes at his shoulders reminded all this was no mere dragoon. He carried with him an old, leather-wrapped horse riding crop tucked under his arm, while at his hip, bulging beneath the lining of his long cavalry coat, the steel of his trusty *couteau de chasse* described a sinister curve. A horsehair periwig, freshly starched, adorned his head, which, in turn, was crowned with a grand black tricorn hat bearing a cockade of pure white silk.

"I see you've started without me," he said, noting the near-empty bottle of beer on the squat table between us, his tone bright and full of life despite its creaky, adenoidal note. "It is unbecoming of a gentleman to drink without a companion. Allow me to remedy that."

The baron drew the barkeep's attention with a casual wave of one finely manicured hand encircled by a cuff of lace at its wrist, and promptly a second glass was brought for the wine.

"You're late," I said. "I'd begun to wonder if you would make our appointment at all or just disappear again like you seem to do."

"Late?" the baron said indignantly. "Munchausen is never late. It is time that's wrong. I always keep a date."

While we waited for the wine to breathe, he struck a match and lit his pipe.

"There is no smoking allowed indoors anymore," I said.

"Yes, I heard something about that." He blinked in between puffs with complete disregard. "An ill-conceived tyranny of morals. To deprive a man of his smoke, and a soldier, especially, is to deprive him of nothing less than his happiness, as well as his sound judgment. It's a well-established fact that no decision of significance or magnitude in the history of mankind was ever reached in a smokeless room."

He sucked the stem of his pipe luxuriously, exuding a long, velvety wisp of vanilla smoke that, to my amazement, drifted not up and over our heads but instead winded downward and slithered like a snake into a hollow tree trunk, disappearing straight into the pocket of his vest.

"I trained them long ago," he said, launching into a memory with a smile. "A skill that has proved its worth on more than one occasion. I was once enjoying the hospitality of a certain wife of the emir of Kokand when His Highness returned suddenly from a battle with the Tajiks. It was assumed by his advisors the fight would not be easy, and he would be away for many weeks. However, victory had proved unexpectedly swift. I was, of course, regaling Her Majesty with some stories of my adventures in the interior of Africa, and was smoking my pipe, as is my fashion, when the emir burst through the front gates at the head of an army ten thousand strong. I was forced to quickly seek shelter in a tremendous wardrobe of solid gold and encrusted with diamonds and other precious stones while the cuckold searched the palace high and low, convinced of his wife's infidelity. He was a most distrustful and paranoid fellow, this emir, consumed by jealousy, and tore the place fairly apart looking for his usurper. And he'd have found me, too, had providence not interceded. As it happened, I'd just finished a month-long regimen of training my fog in the manner you have just observed, so the evidence of my presence was well concealed from both sight and smell. If not for it, there is little doubt the emir would have discovered me and taken my head."

I pointed out the smoking bans were less about preserving decorum and more about protecting the general health and welfare of others. He'd have little of it.

"I have enjoyed at least one pipe every day these last two hundred and eighty-one years, and you will witness it has not been to the detriment of my constitution. In fact, as I have already explained, it has saved my head more times than I can count."

"Not everyone has the luxury of enjoying a physique as robust as your own," I said.

"This is true," he concurred. "I have been blessed, if it can be put that way."

"Then you would also agree the ill effects of your smoke would naturally be a hazard to any without your good fortune."

"Which is why I went to such pains to train them. I can contain the offensive exhaust here and release it later where it doesn't bother anyone. It's quite simple, and I'd a plan to enact the practice on a national scale, but as is often the case in this strange country of yours, one or two holdouts in your Congress scuttled the entire enterprise. In its place, an abolition, sanctioned by the few and imposed on the whole. A curious result for a land touting itself home to free men. But not one without precedent, I suppose. Yours is a most litigious society. You bicker over your own laws with each other almost as frequently as you make war with others over theirs."

"Voltaire said the only perfect laws were the ones made for gaming."

"Leave it to a Frenchman to state the obvious," he said flatly, tamping the bowl of his pipe methodically with two slender gray fingers.

"We aren't without our shortcomings," I said.

"Nor your ironies," the baron clucked. "They are as multifarious as they are multitudinous. I can tell you, sir, I have learned firsthand just what things both wonderful and terrifying are to be beheld in this America of yours."

A twinkle flashed in the old man's eye. It wasn't hard for him to see the anticipation building inside me. I could do little to hide it. It was what I'd been waiting months to hear. The unvarnished truth straight from the horse's mouth. He leaned forward, beckoning me to do the same with a conspiratorial nod.

"Those stories they've been telling about me in the news?" he said, gesturing toward the television behind the bar. "Those are only the ones they let me tell. The ones they wanted everyone to hear. The others, well . . ."

He reclined back into the folds of his chair, an amused smirk playing about his pale lips, leaving me hunched over the table like a fool. I knew instantly he would not be so forthcoming. An old boaster only plies his trade to a willing audience, lest there be no fuel for his fire. There was no choice but to pick up the bait left so blatantly before me. To get the full story, I would have to appeal to his vanity. Assuming a woefully transparent air of nonchalance, I took the bottle in hand and poured out the wine.

"How many years has it been?" I asked. "Ten? Twenty?"

"Not since Munich, I imagine," Munchausen said. "I do forget the odd encounter from time to time. Not to belittle our friendship in any way, mind you. It's just I've had so many adventures. Three hundred years is a long time to keep everything straight. You can forgive me the occasional lapse in memory."

"I'm flattered you would consider us friends," I said.

"You should be. It is not a term I bandy about lightly. I have had many admirers, and even more respectful enemies, but few I could call friends."

"Why is that, do you suppose?"

"I attribute it mainly to the cause of philosophy. Rational thought and I have rarely found ourselves on the same sides of the battlefield, though I daresay you won't find a man more irrational in his thinking than I. It has always been the perceptions of others I've found excessively troubling. Reconciling Munchausen against the rigid systems of objectivism, materialism, or idealism is something most are quite incapable of. Personally, I blame Kant for it, though Descartes is not without fault either. Men have forever been knocking their brains against the sides of their skulls to try and figure out just how I do it. But there's no real secret. I am Hieronymus Karl Friedrich, Baron von Munchausen. I do; therefore, I exist. Conversely, I exist; therefore, I do. Like a metaphor, or a line of poetry, the existing is found in the image, not the act. Samuel Johnson understood this. Your Samuel Clemens too. Those were men of vision. Come to think of it, perhaps further research is warranted into why Samuels are more open to the possibilities of time than those with other names. They say the Samuel of the Bible was a seer of sorts. Maybe there was some truth to it after all. Nevertheless, philosophy is such an ancient curse, and we'd do well to avoid its pitfalls here."

"Doubters shouldn't be dismissed for their skepticism," I said. "It's human nature."

"But neither should they be countenanced for their impunity, or their lack of critical insight. With them, it is always how. *How* Munchausen this, and *how* Munchausen that. Like a blind sword swallower, they always miss the point."

"I'm not following," I said.

"The question to ask is not *how* Munchausen, but *why* Munchausen."

I admit, the query left me at a loss. The baron, perhaps sensing blood in the water, arched a curious eyebrow and pressed the attack.

"Have you yourself never thought to marvel at the sheer preposterousness of it all? Ask yourself, why does the woodpecker beat its head so violently against a tree trunk to dig out a meal when there are plenty of perfectly good insects to be found just wandering about free for the picking? Strictly speaking, and no disrespect to the woodpecker intended, the behavior is ludicrous and wholly unnecessary, but does the bird care? No, yet he beats his brains silly all the same. And what about the whale (or even the dolphin, for that matter), an animal that must breathe air to survive, yet lives in the one place on Earth where there is none to be found. Think about it. A creature living almost its entire life holding its breath. The thing itself is the very definition of madness."

"You're speaking of natural phenomena, the product of millions of years of evolution. Those things couldn't be any other way than they are. A whale just can't get tired of holding its breath and decide to move out of the ocean onto dry land."

"And why not?" Munchausen asked with all the gravity of a man defending the very principles upon which he has built his life. "The decision is his to make, not yours. When he's ready, he'll make the move. I have seen a fox leap right out of its own skin, bones and all, after its tail got nailed to a tree, just as sure as I have witnessed newly free men willfully return to the lands of their own captivity rather than go home, so accustomed had they become to the lifestyle of a slave. You would not classify these as natural phenomena, would you? Yet they happened all the same. It is only because of your rational mind that you find them so troubling to believe. The average brain is too grounded in facts and figures and the mundaneness of what passes for reality these days, too taxed in seeking the genuine. My mind, however, is not bound to these nonfictive anchors. Munchausen is free, then, to explore life with fancy, if not the occasional flight, both literal and figurative, mind you, and see it for what it really is. A revelation of truth, even if expressed in a terminological inexactitude, as Churchill once so eloquently categorized it, remains a truth, nonetheless. Rationality seeks only to discourage the existence of that same truth, because it cannot reconcile itself to the logic of it. But it remains truth all the same, no matter how absurd it may seem. So, you see, *how* is quite irrelevant. *Why* Munchausen? Why? Because it could be no other. Desperate times call for fictive measures, and all that and such."

The baron sipped his wine contentedly and turned his gaze to the fiery majesty of an oval red beryl set in silver adorning his pinky finger. On the television, a fury of coarse words flowed between Laura Ingraham and Katie Couric. Apparently, a discord over the exact number of Spaniards slain by the baron at the siege of Gibraltar. An iron cage was at that moment being erected at John Marshall Park, where the ladies had agreed to settle the matter in gladiatorial fashion.

"So, you admit, then, your stories are fictions?" I said.

"Only as much as life is an unending series of fictions masquerading as realities. And the laws of a fictitious reality must be based on that same fiction. As a rational man, you could no more interpret those laws as you could open up a volume of David Copperfield and step into the shoes of Uriah Heep. The ratiocination is rejected on its premise. But not so for Munchausen, who, as you also know, does not concern himself with fatuity. The whale will walk among us and breathe fresh mountain air when the fancy strikes him; it is all but guaranteed. I have seen much stranger things than this, I tell you, and many right here in your own country. But I don't suppose you invited me here to listen to a lecture. You'd much rather hear what it is that I've learned observing your fellow countrymen these last months. What nuggets of wisdom has Munchausen unearthed in the land of the free and home of the brave? It is, after all, why you've asked me here, isn't it?"

I refreshed his glass of Malbec by way of response, and a delightful sparkle flashed in the corner of the old man's eye.

"Just remember," he began. "Upon my honor, I have only, and will only continue to confine myself to the facts."

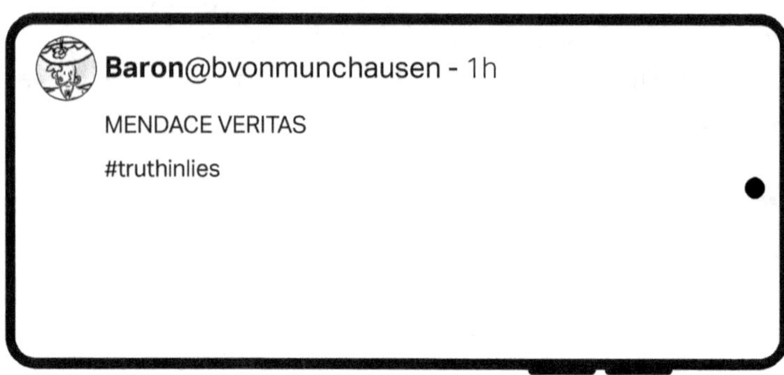

CHAPTER I

It had been some time since I'd set foot on Earth, and in point of fact, I'd no real intention of coming back. For well-nigh a hundred years, I'd been living in comfort and quietude among the inhabitants of the moon—a glorious, if not sublimely industrious, people.

The current king of the moon, Azkabarbar III—whose grandfather's acquaintance I'd had the pleasure of making on my second sojourn there round about 1757—had long since abandoned his line's hopeless war with the peoples of the sun, thus bringing about an extended age of enlightenment for one and all. As it happens, perpetuating a conflict against the only society in the solar system upon which your own civilization is almost wholly dependent for its energy source, just because you don't approve of the way they dress, is not exactly a productive way to foster meaningful interstellar relationships. Perhaps a testament to all futile conflicts raged by despots hoping to bring themselves fame by tilting at the windmills of intangible foes, the young regent's reversal of nearly two hundred years of forced conscription allowed his people to give over their energies to more aesthetic pursuits. Without the threat of imprisonment hanging over their heads, the citizens of Lunolongo—the chief and capital city of the moon, for those not savvy—took to the arts, philosophy, and the humanities with gusto, turning out fantastic wonders of architecture like the Mzgarbak Bridge and the magnificent Frluntsktoop, an edifice rising nearly ten miles into the sky and constructed entirely from the bones of the lunar bull, an animal I need not remind you is of prodigious size.*

The philosopher Hnzgralbuk was at this time working on his now famous treatise, *An Examination of the Birth of Vapor in Closed Vessels*, which finally put to rest a debate that had been raging through lunar society for some four hundred years and had caused no small amount of violence. As you know, water is a commodity in short supply on the moon, so the normally mundane task of boiling a kettle to make a cup of tea is not undertaken lightly. Generally, a committee of civic authorities must be convened before the first leaf is steeped. The matter to be determined: exactly when a pot of water can be said to have reached its boiling point—specifically, is it when the first molecules of water form bubbles of vapor at the floor of the kettle, or when they emerge from the surface of the liquid and enter the atmosphere? If, by some random act of nature, the vapor failed

---

* Author's note: It was here I felt compelled to interrupt the baron's narrative to inquire as to exactly why, if such tremendous structures existed on the moon, the scientific community of Earth had never been able to view them? What with satellites and even several lunar landings (both manned and unmanned) in the previous fifty years, how is it an entire civilization could remain undetected by even the most basic observations? Any ten-year-old with a twenty-dollar backyard telescope should be able to see them.

Annoyed by my interruption, as well as the intrusion of what he referred to as my "hopeless" rationale, the baron leveled his gaze and replied, "It should be obvious to even someone with a brain as simple as that same ten-year-old's that the easiest way to avoid being seen is to move to a place one cannot be seen. In the case of lunar society, that meant moving *inside* the moon. It's hollow, you know, as are a surprising number of moons and planets in our solar system. I'd certainly tell you more about this intriguing phenomenon if we had more time, but as it is, I am endeavoring to confine my narrative to only my experiences in America, and I would thank you in advance for not interrupting me further."

to reach the surface after its formation, could it then be said to be vapor at all, or just an anomalous property of the water itself? Was a person, once having undertaken the process of heating the water, obligated to see it all the way through to its boiling?

Hnzgralbuk finally put the question to rest once and for all when he proved beyond all doubt it was not the will of vapor to come into existence at all; rather, it only formed as a result of the action of someone bringing it to be. And since environmental factors like elevation and ambient humidity, too, played a part in their formation, which would again suggest it was the water itself determining its own decision to boil or not, it was absurd to lay the entire responsibility on the shoulders of the person who just, after all, wanted a simple cup of tea. Therefore, the question of when vapor forms was ultimately the decision of the vapor itself, and since no one up to that point had thought to ask it whether or not it wanted to exist in the first place, the entire debate was moot. When objections were raised—specifically, as to the method of how one is supposed to communicate with water either in its liquid or its vaporous state, water at the time being understood to be insentient, and Hnzgralbuk suggested all efforts be placed in determining just such a method—people gave the whole argument up and just decided to drink the tea.

With lunar society thriving culturally, philosophically, industrially, and agriculturally, I decided to make my home among these good people of the moon. Though it had been some 190-odd years since my last visit, I discovered I still recalled much of their language. Settling in thus proved effortless, and despite my diminutive stature and inability to remove my head from my body at will (the Lunarians, as I have related in the past, are well over twenty feet tall and possess the unique gift of self-decapitation, which has served them to some advantage), I was warmly welcomed into the community. Shortly thereafter, His Majesty the king sent an emissary to offer me the position of ronzploff mirgblod, which roughly translates to *grand high regent of the Southern Lunar Hemisphere*, a post that I happily accepted.

I made it the first duty of my office to set the people to work constructing a new library, grander than had ever been seen on Earth or the moon before, which they did with amazing assiduousness. I summoned all the preeminent lunar architects, of which there were hundreds, and in short order, plans were drawn up and construction complete. Never before had such a monument to letters been erected. Made entirely of blue moonstone and standing two hundred stories tall, it covers an area twice the size of the whole of Vatican City and consists of no fewer than fifty thousand separate galleries. The building was of such colossal density, it caused a temporary disruption to the moon's natural oscillation. For three days and nights, it swayed on its axis like a pendulum until it adjusted itself to its new burden.

The Munchausen Athenaeum, so named in my honor, would house copies of every lunar text ever set down on paper, as well as several examples of the finest literature the Earth had ever produced. I made several clandestine trips to the world's greatest libraries—incognito, of course—to collect works for translation and printing in editions five feet tall. From the Bibliothèque nationale in Paris, I took the Gutenberg Bible, and from the British Library, a First Folio. Copernicus, Aristotle, Newton, Augustine of Hippo, and countless others too. In all, I brought back the original texts of five thousand books, all of which remain in the lunar library to this day.

My term as grand high regent saw the completion of many other projects like this, all with the aim of improving lunar culture. But as time wore on, I grew weary of the responsibilities of my office, and I respectfully tendered my resignation to the king. For my faithful service, he had a palace built for me overlooking the lava sea of Fnuzl, where I could retire in peace and enjoy my days in study and solitude.

I'd had plans to begin recording my thoughts for a volume regarding the role of the leaf beetle in the collapse of the Roman Empire and was hard at it one day behind my desk when my doorman knocked and announced the arrival of a curious visitor.

My guest wore a broad-brimmed petasos of vibrant royal blue

tied tight under his chin that concealed the upper half of his face. A matching chlamys, like a crystalline waterfall, cascaded over his bronzed shoulders and muscular torso. A pair of leather sandals shod his feet, each sprouting a pair of golden eagle's wings. I recognized him immediately as none other than Hermes, the fleet-footed messenger of the gods.

"To what do I owe this pleasure?" I asked, already knowing a journey now lay ahead of me. One is not visited by a messenger god unless it is to be summoned to appear.

"There has been a request," he began, his voice soft yet resonant, like the sound of a bell being rung underwater. "An invitation extended."

"I am needed on Olympus again?" I said. "My God, what need have the gods of Munchausen? I am just an old man trying to enjoy his last days in peace."

"Not Olympus. Earth."

"Earth? What need does it have for me?"

"I am but the messenger," he said, a trite, if not obvious, retort. He drew near and handed me the folded parchment from beneath his cape, a letter that he'd been commanded by the universe to deliver. It read as follows:

BARON HIERONYMOUS VON MUNCHAUSEN,
We need you.

The note was signed only: *a concerned citizen of the United States of America.*

"What shall I return as a reply?" Hermes inquired.

Without any delay, I dismissed the divine courier, giving him leave to return to Olympus. I had decided I would not be much of a Munchausen if I did not respond in person, and quickly gathering my pistols, fusil, and a few other items I deemed necessary for the voyage, I set off at once for Earth.

"I now know, of course, it was you who sent the message," Munchausen said. "A concerned citizen indeed."

"I figured an invitation would be difficult to resist," I replied. "The soldier in you would be hard-pressed to decline an open plea for aid from a people in need. Admit it, if you knew it was just me asking, you would not have come otherwise."

The baron drew in a tranquil measure of smoke up the stem of his pipe and exhaled it through a slit in the corner of a crooked grin, the bulging knot of his Adam's apple beneath the translucent skin of his gaunt neck bobbing lazily like a cork on the waves.

"What need does America today have of Munchausen, eh? Is there not enough irrationality to go around that you need to add mine to the pot to spice up the broth?"

"More than enough," I said. But that's the problem. It has become so bad, we can't see the forest for the trees.

"So now you're speaking for an entire nation, is that it? Quite an audacious strategy. I shudder to imagine what your fellow countrymen might think of you taking the reins in this fashion. Censure will undoubtedly follow."

"And that is just part of the problem," I agreed. "No one is free to say what they mean anymore without fear of condemnation. It's like the lunatics are running the asylum."

"Who better to ridicule the ridiculous, is that it?"

I nodded my approval. The baron clucked his tongue by way of reply.

"Still, you're here all the same," I said, attempting to placate him. "My request must have struck some chord in your fictitious heart."

"Only a flat," the baron blandly replied. "No, it was duty that obligated me. I was offered a commission. And, once a soldier . . . well, you see."

CHAPTER II

Once called, neither a soldier nor a gentleman can countenance delay. I set off directly for the Munchausen Athenaeum.

To affect the journey, I first needed to consult a volume of Galileo I'd had installed in the Fragrantia Annex, so named for that lady of inestimable divineness whose heart I'd had the humble pleasure of captivating (how long ago was it now?), so as to deduce the current phase of the moon. As might be expected, one quickly loses track of these things when standing on the lunar surface.

A brief review of the master's *Sidereus Nuncius*, followed by cross-referencing a calendar, showed fortune was on my side. The date was the fifth of October, and the moon would be firmly in its waxing crescent—optimal conditions upon which to embark.

With haste, I informed the king I would be departing on a diplomatic mission of some importance. His Highness was both saddened by my leave-taking but also delighted I should be called to undertake ambassadorial duties on his behalf. You see, ever since you lot had set foot on the surface of the moon, planting flags, kicking up the dust, and otherwise making a mess of what was a meticulously cultivated royal rock garden, His Lunarship had developed a keen interest in just what was going on down here. So, as a condition of my leave, I was doubly charged with the task of keeping a record of my journey for His Majesty that would later be installed in the athenaeum for all to enjoy. I, of course, happily acceded to this request, and thus charged, His Highness made available for me his fastest chariot harnessed to a team of fifty of his swiftest horses, with the result that I was whisked with rapidity from the capital to the lunar north pole some four thousand miles away, the entire trip taking no more than an hour.

No sooner had I arrived than I peered southward across the glistening sands of the white thumbnail of the waxing moon extending before me, a near-perfect arc. And lying beyond the southern tip, past the inky field of glistening stars, the shimmering blue and verdure hues of the celestial marble that is the Earth hung peacefully in the blackness.

Wasting no time, I dismounted my chariot and nestled myself on the pearly ground, using a rock to brace my feet against the severe lunar curvature lest I slip free before I was properly seated. But when the moment came, I kicked the rock aside and rapidly began sliding southward along the thin arc of ground illuminated by the sun, and after building up tremendous speed, I ricocheted over the moon's south pole and was flung full bore like a pebble from a sling up and out into the void.

I left the weak pull of the moon's gravity and quickly became aware that, without proper ballast to steady myself, which, in my haste to leave, I'd forgotten to bring, my uncontrollable tumbling would surely upset my trajectory, which it did, and as I watched the Earth sail by, I found myself hopelessly off course. I might have even been bound to rocket through infinity forever had I not the good fortune to just then pass by the watchful centaur of the sky, Sagittarius, who, seeing me in no small amount of distress, was kind enough to pluck me from my predicament and place me astride one of his arrows. This I clung on with all my strength. And when I signaled I was ready, he leveled his starry bow, and both arrow and I zoomed back toward Earth at an amazing speed.

When I felt myself close enough and sure of my reentry, I released the celestial missile, which is surely still piercing the heavens, probably in the vicinity of the Crab Nebula by now, and began a descending arc toward the planet's surface.

About a thousand feet above the upper reaches of the atmosphere, I suddenly remembered that without some extra weight, I would just graze off the surface like a stone skipping across a lake and be flung back out into space. Luckily, at just that moment, I was able to grab hold of a passing communications satellite. Straddling it as I would a horse, I became heavy enough to continue my descent. But not without some discomfort, mind you, as twice I bounced across the shell of the Earth with such jarring force as to cause a hurricane just then passing east-west over the Atlantic Ocean to turn north-south, thus sparing the island of Martinique from certain destruction. Rapidly, the air grew denser as I approached the surface. This, however, did little to arrest my descent, and I was now sailing directly toward the ground at a frightening pace. The frigid wind streaking past my face drew frozen tears from the corners of my eyes, which rained down like hailstones over the sands of the Kalahari, confusing monkey and man alike, who, as you know, are unfamiliar with the sight of ice in those parts. Squinting against the force of the air, I sought out a means of slowing my fall. From that altitude, I could read the outline of the land sprawled before me as if I were reading a map on a table in my study. I gained my bearings and was quickly able to perceive the isthmus of Central America connecting the northern and southern continents rapidly approaching over the horizon, as well as the peninsula of Florida. South America being off to my left, I ascertained I was hurtling directly toward the southwest part of the United States, specifically the vicinity of Albequerque, New Mexico. It was then I observed a multitude of tiny colorful dots speckling the landscape below like bubbles, which, as I fell closer, I recognized as dozens of hot-air balloons drifting on the wind.

Discarding the satellite, which I made sure to push off toward the sea, I steadied myself and aimed directly for the first balloon available. Newton's laws being immutable, the force of my impact caused the balloon to first contract, then expand in relation to my presence, the effect being I was bounced four miles back up into the air until, gravity seeking its share, I fell back onto the cushion of a second balloon, and then another, and another, losing speed incrementally with each rebound until, through these means, all my velocity was spent and I landed back on terra firma. A most dynamic start to my adventures, if it can be said so. And to think, it wasn't even spring!

"I see not even Munchausen is immune to the great pestilence of the twenty-first century. Really, Baron, a social media account? That's a bit too gauche, even for you."

"Not as much as you employing such ridiculous terms for your own literary edification. I am merely conforming to conventions, whereas you seek to eschew them in pursuit of some higher principle. But in doing so, you forget: a Munchausen's first duty is to the truth. What would fiction be without it? If the medium is the message, as the saying goes, I much prefer my messages rare. Ever since old Gutenberg made that first strike of lead type on parchment, people have sought out ever new and exciting means to broadcast their own personal brand of truth. I even tried my hand at it once. I started a small press of my own in Hamburg, with an imprimatur from His Holiness the Pope himself. This was many, many years ago, mind you."

"Which Pope would that be?"

"The one at the Vatican, of course. Now stop interrupting."

CHAPTER III

Suffice it to say, my unusual entrance raised quite the commotion among both spectator and aeronaut alike, and it was not long before murmurs spread out across the region: Munchausen had made his arrival.

Fame, as Byron once said, is the thirst of youth. I myself have never sought the stuff, yet I cannot seem to escape it. I'd hardly expected such a reception, seeing as how it had been almost one hundred years since last I was among people, and even longer since I'd been across the ocean to your side of the world. Yet my reputation had evidently preceded me all the same.*

Seized with a kind of frenzy, journalists and camera crews—already on-site to record for posterity the annual international ballooning

---

* Author's note: I was forced to admit at this point that much of the anticipation built up around the baron's arrival could be attributed to a robust advertising campaign across the Deep South and Midwest of evangelical roadside billboards I'd had erected along all the major interstates. It turns out "Got Munchausen?" is just as vacuous as "Got Jesus?" and nearly as effective.

It also turns out that people are only too willing to give their money to intentionally vague GoFundMe campaigns.

festivities—turned their collective peepers on yours truly. Descending upon me like a swarm of locusts, they became less like men and more like pieces of human artillery. Questions blasted from the barrels of their mouths like verbal grapeshot. I could do little at first but dodge the flying bits of grammar and implore the mass to compose a semblance of order and direct their queries one at a time. Alas, my warning came too late, for one unfortunate reporter from the *San Francisco Chronicle* was killed outright in the fray, impaled through the back by a stray fragment of particularly prickly syntax.

"Baron! What are your thoughts on universal health care?"

"The universe is quite healthy, I can assure you, save for a mild case of background radiation. But I'm sure it will pass."

"They're finding swarms of murder hornets in Oregon. What's to be done about it?"

"Prosecute them to the fullest extent of the law, I say. A civilized society simply cannot tolerate murderers roaming free in the streets."

"If a tree falls in the woods and there's no one to hear it, does it *really* make a sound?"

"If there's no one there to hear it, how would you know it fell? I recall hunting grouse in the forests of Normandy one summer when, through the underbrush, my ears were met with the distinct sobs of what I could only assume to be a lost child. Rushing toward the source of the sound, I was amazed to find it coming not from a wandering babe but rather from a weeping willow mourning the loss of its friend, who'd burned down the night before. The poor elm, it seemed, was the victim of an unfortunate lightning strike."

"Do you think we'll ever know who really killed Kennedy?"

"Well, that was clearly the CIA. Isn't that obvious?"

"What do you think of the recent push by candidates on the right calling for the restoration of law and order?"

"Well I've never been one to go in for crime procedurals. I've always been more of a traditional sitcom man myself. *Cheers, All in the Family, Ozzie and Harriet*, that sort of thing."

"Why have you returned now?"

"Was I not asked?"

"Where have you come from?"

"Would it not be more prudent to ask where I am going?"

"All right, then. Where *are* you going?"

"Does anyone really know where they are going? You know, Don Quixote once told me—"

Suddenly, and with no little trepidation, the crowd of reporters and onlookers parted like the Red Sea before Moses as a delegation of serious-looking officers in olive-green fatigues marched their way directly through the group. Heavily armored, and bearing even heavier arms, they insinuated their authority with sobering menace from behind their black sunglasses. Then their lieutenant stepped forward.

"I have it on good authority that you have entered this country illegally, sir. Let's see some ID. Where are your papers?"

"Papers?" I replied. "It's been long since I've had recourse to return to the confines of two-dimensional spaces. A terribly limiting type of existence, that. I much prefer three dimensions, or four or five. Live in a two-dimensional world, and one's thinking tends to become as flat as the pages of a book; you never see past the deckled edge. No, sir, I've no need of papers. A man is defined by actions, not words on a page."

"Without proper identification verifying your legal status, you cannot be in the United States. We have laws here, sir," the lieutenant replied rigidly.

"As do I," I said. "The Munchausens are an honorable and law-abiding people down to the last man. I never met a law I dared break. Every action I have ever taken has always been within the confines of natural law. Take, for example, the law of probability. It should go without saying that my sudden and unannounced presence in your country would bring a significant amount of attention to bear. It could not possibly have escaped yours. Now, suppose, in this instance, we were to quantify that amount of attention, assigning it a value N. Now, Laplace's ninth principle states quite clearly, in a line of probable events, where some produce a benefit (in this case,

E+1) and others a loss (E-1), if the sum of those events producing a probable benefit outnumbers the sum of those events producing a probable loss, then hope, being a constant, shall remain as an attainable outcome. Conversely, should the reverse be true, that the probable losses outweigh the probable benefits, hope then becomes a variable. Left unchecked, it inevitably becomes fear. Let me pause here and ask, you are familiar with Laplace, aren't you? I hope I have not lost you?"

The lieutenant shifted uneasily in his heavy boots. Dozens of reporters, their phone cameras trained on his face, waited eagerly for a reply.

"Of course?" he said, more a question than an answer. "But go on, if it makes you feel better."

"Splendid! Now, assuming our meeting is the final event in the series of events beginning with my receiving of an invitation to come to your great land, then we can surmise, as you and I had not encountered each other until this day, that the number of events benefitting me, E+1, must far outweigh the singular loss of your demanding my identification, E-1. Therefore, the attention garnered by my presence could be expressed thusly: $N = (E+1) - (E-1)$. Correct?"

"Okay."

"So, the only logical conclusion to be drawn is that hope indeed remains and fear is nowhere to be seen. And since I am not afeard of my lack of papers, they must therefore be wholly unnecessary, and I can be on my way."

Flummoxed yet duty bound, the lieutenant remained stone-faced. His fellow officers appeared equally unmoved, utterly ignorant of the fact that the tide had already turned against them.

"None of that matters," the lieutenant said, his voice rising in octave, parallel with his annoyance. "Without identification, you're still here illegally, and at this time, you are being placed into custody."

"Ah, now, it is you who is in violation of the law," I astutely observed.

"I know the law, sir."

"I disagree," I said. "Have you forgotten about our little friend N? Do you think it would be probable or improbable that the amount of attention surrounding my arrival should play a significant role in the outcome of this meeting? For, as I stated earlier, a Munchausen does not break the law, not even the law of *improbability*, which holds for us untold surprises."

And in accordance with that very same law, which, mathematically speaking, could be expressed as the time, X, it takes for the attention I garnered, N, to travel across the country to the house of the president of the United States and back again, an extremely improbable event occurred. Namely, the telephone in the lieutenant's pocket rang at just that very moment with instructions to cease and desist all attempts to detain me further and escort me at once to Washington, DC, where festivities were already being planned and arrangements made for a grand state banquet reception to be held in my honor.

The small matter of my immigration status at last put to rest, the lieutenant and I became fast friends. I was being advised that air transportation was being arranged forthwith to bring me to the fete when there arose another concern. It already being quite late in the day, there was no possibility of my getting to the capital before sundown. This put the crowd in a state of despair. But I assure you, Munchausen did not despair, and I sought to reassure everyone that all would promptly be set right.

"Fear not," I said. "No Munchausen before me, from my great-great-great-grandfather Gottfried Augustus Fredregar Hildebrand von Munchausen to mine own father, has ever been late, never before in these last seven hundred years, and I don't intend to let my family's renowned streak of punctuality come to ignominious defeat so easily."

How is it that I remained so confident in this assertion you ask? Surely Munchausen, having seen the country from the sky can appreciate the shear vastness of the place. How could he possibly span the distance in time? Shall I tell you?

It so happened that I remembered just then that among the items I had quickly assembled prior to leaving on my journey were a pair of seven-league boots I'd won in a wager with a traveling scholar* in a game of Ruff and Honors some years ago.

My solemn vow to retain the Munchausens' good name thus delivered, the crowd's spirits lifted, and, donning the boots, I said my farewells, with a promise to return, before leaping from the spot almost three miles into the air and landing some fifty miles east. Another step brought me farther still, and in this way, I continued my stroll at a leisurely pace. In just over an hour, my feet came to rest on the grassy sward of the National Mall.

My arrival there, both momentous and unexpected as it was, drew no smaller amount of notice as it had when I'd made my entrance at the balloon festival. Within minutes, I was again besieged by throngs of gawkers, rubberneckers, and shutterbugs, all clambering over each other like so many thousands of ants swarming a morsel of table scrap carelessly discarded on the floor.

As you know, I have never been one to be impressed by celebrity, nor have I ever sought it out for myself. In fact, the life of a soldier should be self-effacing—humble, even. Glory is for the battlefield alone, and when the battle is won, though a story or two remains, a true soldier simply returns to his home and family, their love reward enough for a job well done. All too often have I seen service traded for privilege, and heroics confused with sagacity.

A Munchausen and his vanity are soon parted, as the saying goes, and to extricate myself from the riffraff of photo seekers, I contrived the simplest of solutions. Zooming through the void of the stars, combined with the heat of my atmospheric reentry and the dust gathered on my recent jaunt across the country, had left my shirt, waistcoat, breeches, and stockings in a less-than-fresh state.

---

* Author's note: I asked the baron if he could elaborate further on this so-called scholar, but he shuddered at the mere thought of giving a moment's shrift to this mysterious man, saying only: "Monsieur M. was an individual of many amazing and singular talents, including, but not limited to, being devilishly adept at poker."

In short, I was in no way more presentable for a state dinner than I was for a cannibal's feast and was in desperate need of a launder.

Fortunately, time was on my side. Or, to be more accurate, at my back. For, you see, my recent ride on Sagittarius's celestial missile had a twofold benefit. Firstly, it guided me back on course to Earth. Secondly, having done so at faster than the speed of light, a testament to that archer's otherworldly might, it was necessary then only to wait for the imminent arrival of my past self, who, by my calculations, at that moment should have been stepping over Paducah, Kentucky.

My math was indeed not that far off, and a few seconds later, I spied myself descending from the clouds onto the turf before the gates of the Smithsonian. Once he'd arrived, I apprised my doppelganger of the situation, and he was only too pleased to remain posing for selfies with the crowd to their hearts' content, which, judging by the line forming (it now stretched as far south as Richmond), would not be abating anytime soon.

With this little complication now solved, I took the opportunity to exit discreetly and made for the first dry cleaners I could find so that I might freshen up for dinner.

CHAPTER IV

A freshly pressed coat and a smart shine on one's boots oft puts a man in mind of perambulatory inclinations, and the pleasingly fragrant odor of starch doing much to influence my mood, I made private designs to wander the city at my leisure. However, these plans were dashed almost before they had time to incubate, for as I'd emerged upon the avenue, I was, once again, like Troy before Agamemnon, surrounded by a besieging army—not of common rabble, as before, but rather a brigade of an entirely different stamp. For awaiting me outside the tailor's shop stood a retinue consisting of none other than the president of the United States himself, his entire cabinet of advisors, the full complement of both houses of Congress with their respective aides-de-camp, and no fewer than eleven thousand photographers, commentators, correspondents, and other agents of the press from fifty-three countries come along

---

* Author's note: Sadly, I am completely ignorant when it comes to Latin, whereas it might as well be the baron's second (or is it fifth?) tongue. Later recourse to my own bookshelf led me to Hobbes's *Leviathan*, Book 2, Chapter 26: "Authority, not truth, makes law."

to document the expedition.

The president was the first to speak. With a rehearsed smile and an outstretched hand, he doddered forward uneasily on a pair of spindly appendages resembling more river reeds than legs. Seeing them, I reflected on the stout legs of my patron, His Majesty Azkabarbar the Globate, who, though himself some 5,427 years old, still stood tall and hardy on five legs, each ten meters around and solid as granite columns (the sixth leg having been lost in battle some years before during the siege of Ursa Major). In comparison, this fellow's pillars of state left much to be desired, and I could hardly believe it was upon them that the foundations of the "free" world rested.

The heavy burden of command had wreaked a terrible toll. The commander in chief's weary countenance was positively shocking, and I was equally gobsmacked to learn he was a mere seventy-six years young, by all rights still in the flower of his youth. And you know, for me, who has been permitted to walk this earth for well-nigh three hundred years, with some exceptions that I have previously related, to note a man should appear so old is no small matter. If I have been graced with Methuselah's gift of longevity, then it can also be said I have been equally blessed with Adonis's gift of pulchritude. At 293 years old, I still retain the youthful countenance of a man half my age, whereas this fellow looked positively decrepit. I shuddered to think, if reappointed, what his next four years would bring.

Nonetheless, I endeavored to conduct myself with the decorum befitting a man in his position, tenuous as it was.

"Mr. President," I began after the appropriate pleasantries had been exchanged, "it is truly a splendid honor to be invited to tour your glorious land. As an ambassador of the irrational, it pleases me beyond measure to be afforded the opportunity to experience firsthand the birthplace of modern enlightenment. And as you know me to be a man of veracity, let me be the first to say I attend my duties with both open heart and open mind."

This declaration was met with nods of approbation all around, and an impromptu tour of the city was quickly arranged, whereby

I was promised to be shown some of the wonders of the greatest political system the world has ever known, namely the American democratic process.

Our first stop saw us enter the National Archives, where I was given the opportunity to view the hallowed charters of freedom upon which this land was built and by which its people derive their unequivocal liberties, these consisting primarily of the Declaration of Independence, the Constitution, and the Bill of Rights. We found these documents enshrined in sarcophagi of stone and glass at the base of a grand rotunda of marble and granite whose walls bore magnificent, towering, and idyllic murals more than a dozen feet high.

"And who are they?" I inquired of the figures portrayed.

"Those are the Founding Fathers."

"So many," I noted. "Where are the mothers?"

"These were the giants who framed the very soul of this great country. Men of purpose and vision who saw the rights of all as inviolable."

"And the lefts, what of those?"

This question, like so many I would ask in the coming weeks, would remain curiously unanswered. Instead, a gentle hand at my elbow ushered me forward for a closer inspection of those august documents.

"Quite a high level of security?" I said, noting the armed guards flanking our position.

"Freedom must be protected," a senator chimed in.

"Protected from what?" I asked.

"Why, from those who would take it from us, of course?"

"And who might those be?"

"Freedom has many enemies," the president said. "It always has. Not everyone loves freedom as much as America does."

"Perhaps they merely covet freedom of a different kind?" I posited. "*Quod ali cibus est aliis fuat acre venenum*, as the saying goes. What is food for one may be poison to others."

A general murmur rippled through the crowd and then died a slow death into silence confined within the walls of that granite prison.

"Not a scholar among you, I see?" I said, dismayed yet undeterred. "Allow me to put it in simpler terms, then. Consider, if you will, the dandelion and the bocce—"

"Nonsense." The president chuckled, cutting me short with a polite wave of his hand. "Sir, there is only one kind of freedom, everyone knows that quite well. There's no point in discussing what is and isn't free. A free people know they are free."

"Oh? How do they, exactly?" I asked.

"It's written right here for all to see, of course. Given to all the peoples of this and every land on Earth, whether they want it or not. One doesn't really get to choose one's freedom. One doesn't even need to ask for it. America, as a beacon of light in the darkest night, brings it to one and all regardless. It is, after all, what our founders intended."

"So I have heard," I said. "Correct me if I am mistaken, but is it not the moth who seeks out the flame and not the other way around? After all, it's them whose wings get singed."

An acceding murmur rose among a contingent of journalists hailing from the Middle East. They raised several hands, imploring me to expound further. In fact, I had just begun to relate an interesting anecdote from a trip I took to the Hindu Kush when the president energetically seized me by the elbow and hurriedly rushed us out of that hallowed hall and on to our next destination.

A brief promenade past the Capitol building brought us to the chambers of the Supreme Court, where my presence proved a particularly fortuitous boon for those esteemed magistrates, who were embroiled in a most peculiar case, one that, for all their precedents, they were unable to come to a decisive conclusion on.

Relieved at the sight of Munchausen entering their chamber, the illustrious judges, finding themselves deadlocked, petitioned me to step forward and assist in their deliberations. I acceded to their pleas on the sole condition I be given free rein to take whatever measures I deemed necessary to ensure the litigants received a fair and impartial hearing. The request was granted, and I set about commencing my plan.

Taking inspiration from the blind figure of Lady Justice, I drew my *couteau de chasse* and set about removing the eyes from all nine of Their Honors' heads, thus ensuring their impartiality when viewing the facts. There were, of course, objections—this was a court of law after all—and the chief justice himself did attempt to flee, but his flight was overruled by a simple six-to-three majority. This business complete, I then climbed the bench and tossed their chairs on the floor of the gallery. These were hastily dismantled and refashioned into nine thirty-foot-high poles, at the top of which was affixed a seat for each magistrate. Thus installed on these new perches, those nine interpreters of the law were compelled to balance their position by nothing more than their individual ability to sit perfectly still, swaying neither to the left nor to the right lest they come crashing down to certain death. By these means, I hoped to firmly establish each one's utmost neutrality as arguments were presented while simultaneously drawing attention to the, ahem, gravity of the proceedings.

With the justices sorted and situated, I next turned my attention to the litigants. Thousand-dollar suits and imported Italian shoes spoke more about the salaries of these legal eagles than their mindfulness of the peoples' will. The pungent odor of special-interest money punctuated the air around tables on both sides of the aisle, threatening to further corrupt the proceedings. At first, I thought of taking the added precaution of slicing off the justices' noses lest they catch a whiff, but in the end, I settled on casting out all the attorneys posthaste. In their places, I installed new learned counsel to argue the bare facts of the case with the maximum amount of dispassion befitting their roles.

On the side of the petitioner, I called upon the services of the grand orator and statesman Daniel Webster, who, as you know, famously argued to the better of Lucifer himself. With one fist planted firmly on the podium, the other shielding his heart, he opened the arguments.

"Your Honors, if it please the court, or if it doesn't, it matters not, the forthright inviolability of human profligacy, taken as it were, when overmatched, yet not assumed to be complete and unutterable, only when, of course, due diligence has been exaggerated and the heart of the offense has been expurgated, per se, through the filter of ex parte influences, cannot be disputed.

"Assuming a hemispherical approach, consigning all outward genetics to quintessential modes of operation, whilst simultaneously advocating minimal magnitudes, amplified twice, nay, thrice, over by the oppositional forces competing ad nauseam in complete disregard to the rising of universal synergies at play, begs a most thoughtful question. One, Your Honors, I implore you to answer in our favor.

"To view the reflection of the truth, you need look no further than the earthworm. It stands to reason, when matches are lit, the ears of the deaf are the first to burn. Recognizing the fragility of the crystalline flagellations under and within the microcosms of antithetical propositions of similar miens, to assume any other conclusion would be to court folly and ridicule. And so it is in the case. Thank you."

Concluding his remarks thusly, the esteemed orator returned to his seat. I stood in awe of his sublimely labyrinthine assessment of statutory civil law. It was then the turn of the respondent to offer a rebuttal. This task called for an advocate of no less zealousness and verve. I could think of none more qualified in this regard than His Excellency, Grand Inquisitor Tomás de Torquemada, who now rose from his chair, crossed himself thrice, then took the floor.

"Your High Lord and Ladyships, whose circumspect sagacity is matched only by your extreme longevity, I implore you to flagellate yourselves and gird your exceedingly judicious loins against the well-spoken yet woefully inconclusive remonstrances of my distinguished colleague.

"I draw your attention to the facts. It was Erasmus, not Cicero, as the petitioner would have you believe, who said, 'A deaf man went to law with a deaf man: the judge was deafer still.' In light of these prognostications, it cannot be deduced otherwise. Fear, Your Honors, fear of the rule of law, fear of God alone, is paramount. For what are we without fear? Where would man be without fear? What would the American nation be without fear?

"Taking for granted the godless nature of my adversary, one could easily give credence to his beliefs. But God is love, not freedom. God does not concern himself with liberty. And this free society that my esteemed opponent and others like him represent cannot abide the absence of God's loving restrictions on those self-same freedoms he claims to covet so dearly. Reject divine limits? I ask you, where does that leave us? Thank you."

Once the venerated friar had regained his seat, it was time for the justices to deliberate the matter and issue a ruling, one which would stand for all time.

The first to speak was a corpulent originalist who'd been seated on the bench for more than thirty years, and who was nearly as old as the precedents he cited. With grammatical flourish, he began constructing a grand framework to support his argument, founded in the deepest roots of the Constitution. But it was a scaffolding made of obsolete paradigms too flimsy to withstand the gusts of modern sentiment, and in a flash, he toppled from his perch with such astonishing speed as to cause the two on either side of him to come crashing down as well, killing all three in the process, their necks snapping beneath the crushing weight of their judicial suppositions.

The next to offer an opinion, a judge known for her liberal inclinations, sought to find common ground between the parties involved. Vacillating wildly between moral conservatism and secular humanism, she cast so broad a utilitarian net that sadly she, too, tumbled overboard and drowned beneath the waves of her own sophistry.

Seeing the fate of established law left on tenuous footing, I resolved to settle the matter myself. Taking measure of the anticipation of those in attendance, I paced methodically before the bench, knitting my brow and pulling at the tip of my beard to draw my thoughts to their sharpest point. When finally I was ready, a general hush settled over the gallery, and I made my pronouncement.

"Gentleman and ladies of the court, familiar as I am with the specious nature of so-called universal laws, the facts of this case appear quite simple to me. It is only left to ask if it is, proverbially speaking, darkest before the dawn. The applicants have both presented compelling cases, and it would be easy to err on the side of caution and let things go along as they may. After all, it is no small feat for us today, with our modern conventions and present scientific and social understanding, to ascertain just what the framers intended when they wrote 'shall' but not 'should' all those centuries ago. But Munchausen does not abide conventions, at least, not when one is in town. So, I will conclude these proceedings by saying it behooves each and every individual to chart their own destiny. Today's liberal is tomorrow's conservative, and yesterday's tyrant tomorrow's messiah. Just as a leopard cannot change its spots, so, too, we cannot upend change for stability. Therefore, I rule, all else being equal, you can, in fact, compare apples to oranges. Judgment for the state, *in pari materia, post hoc ergo propter hoc*, etc. . . ."

"You know, Baron, I read somewhere you've been somewhat of an inspiration for both Nietzsche *and* Wittgenstein?"

"More reference than revelation, in my estimation," he replied. That's always been the problem with people like you, followers of the philosophes. Reading too much into a thing. Searching for a single molecule in all that hot air, when you'd be better off just letting the whole lot of it float away."

"I'd have thought a man, especially one of your particular nature, would want to encourage reading, whether too much or too little, at all cost. I mean, what would become of you if everyone just stopped reading altogether?"

"From what I hear and what I've seen, that is a question of peculiar import around here these days. And a troubling trend, I would add."

"It would certainly spell the death of you."

The baron paused exceedingly long to contemplate this, all the while wistfully shaking his head.

"It's something no one really thinks about, is it?" he said finally. "The death of character. You take a volume off the shelf. Dust off the cover. Crack open the spine, and then, voilà, out it all spills: man, myth, moral. Close it again, toss it back on the shelf, and you cast it all back into the abyss of memory, where it is quickly forgotten, usurped, as it were, by the next newfangled technological distraction. Yet it's not just the dramatis persona that's supplanted. His ideas often die with him. And the death of an idea is a most terrible tragedy."

"Sadly," I said, "it's all too common. My fellow countrymen fear new ideas in general and are quick to dismiss reading for that very reason, among others. It doesn't bode well for you, I'm afraid."

"It's not Munchausen's death you should fear. I have been dead many times before and will die many more, my boy. But stop reading? That would surely be the death of us all."

CHAPTER V

Not twenty-four hours had passed after my pronouncement came down before no fewer than thirty-seven state legislatures had convened (mostly in midnight sessions) to alter their constitutions while their constituents slept. By dawn, interracial marriage was outlawed in ten states, seven militia groups previously listed as terrorist organizations had been legally deputized, and some sixteen thousand teenagers were arrested for not doing their homework. In Wisconsin, it became a crime to mispronounce the governor's name. In Alabama, every household was now required to fly an American flag from their front porch. Texas, now unfettered by that pesky Eighth Amendment, commenced death-row executions with remarkable speed.

In short, the constitutional system was working perfectly.

With thorny legal matters laid to rest, there were events of larger import at hand.

The nation's capital was abuzz with activity. Folks came from far and wide, numbering in the low millions, by my reckoning, to catch a glimpse of the famed baron and see him off on his grand sojourn.

In every corner of the city, parades and concerts celebrated the return of Munchausen.

Columns of schoolchildren in feathered tricorns marched down Massachusetts Avenue to the rousing canticle of "Der Puppenherr." Though they'd had little time to prepare, sculptors and stonemasons commissioned for the occasion wasted none of it erecting no less than two hundred new statues around the city in my honor. In short order, and with remarkable precision, the imposing figure of Lincoln was unseated from his ceremonial chair overlooking the National Mall and a likeness of myself installed in his place (old Honest Abe having been temporarily relocated to an undisclosed location until such time as a new home for him could be found).

Playhouses across the city, including the Kennedy Center, Ford's Theatre, and the National Theatre staged productions of my various victories over the Turk, while outdoors, a recreation of my triumph over the Spanish at Gibraltar along the banks of the Potomac River brought about the unfortunate sinking of nearly two dozen pleasure boats out to observe the occasion. Mercifully, the loss of life was minimal. There was even talk of draining the Tidal Basin so a replica of my lunar villa might be erected for all to experience. Sadly, time constraints forbade the undertaking.

Neither the White House nor its South Lawn, normally the arena reserved for the receiving of high officials of state and other dignitaries, was deemed adequate to accommodate the nearly ten thousand presidents, international potentates, senators, representatives, governors, mayors, magistrates, ministers, councilmen, officials, deputy officials, assistant deputy officials, lawyers, judges, authors, artists, clerks, accountants, celebrities, and other attendees who comprised the guest list for that evening's official state reception. In the end, a stretch of the National Mall between Fourteenth Street and the Capitol Reflecting Pool was annexed for the purpose, and a towering pavilion stitched entirely together out of only the finest imported silks from Vietnam, Malaysia, and Bangladesh two hundred feet high and nearly a mile long was erected on the site. So much

of the stuff had been used, in fact, that the unfortunate women of those countries were recently informed they'd have to wait at least six months or more before going to the shops to buy any new dresses or handbags, stockpiles of the precious fabric having been entirely depleted.

I entered this magnificent tent to the harmony of a thousand choirs singing the praises of the angels and was given the seat of honor at the highest table. At my right hand sat the president of the United States, and at his right hand, the vice president, and at his right, the secretary of state, and so on and so on so that to each's right there sat the individual of the next highest import, whereas to my left hand were seated all the presidents and monarchs of the 195 nations of the world according to their alphabetical rank. At the remainder of the tables, numbering in the hundreds, sat attendees comprised of dignitaries, VIPs, and the like, representing various corporations, financial institutions, universities, and the church, too numerous to count. Those whom the pavilion could not accommodate, and there were many, looked on from outside, observing the proceedings on a tremendous projection screen four hundred feet high and just as wide that stretched from the peak of the Washington Monument.

The ensuing feast bore culinary representation from every land: Haitian squash soup, Canadian butter tarts, plov from the rugged mountains of Azerbaijan, laplap from the far-flung shores of Vanuatu, goat dumplings from the windswept Mongolian steppe. World leaders, who otherwise had no cause to share a table, sampled cuisines so exotic and palate pleasing, they forged hundreds of new trade agreements on the spot and immediately ceased hostilities in three ongoing wars.

Amid this convivial atmosphere, it should come as no surprise that between the fish course and the cheese, the zephyrs of rhetorical fancy swept a tempest over the rocky coastline of my heart. With humble gratitude, I rose to give voice to my thoughts.

"My friends," I began, "who among us can claim immunity from the ruminative qualities digestion imposes upon the mind? Its effects have been illuminated time and again by both science and history. One need look no further than the Gospel of Mark. It couldn't be any plainer. For there, it is written, after fasting in the desert for forty days, Jesus went up the mount and delivered his famous commentary. Impossible, no? Munchausen has gone batty, you say? Shall we inquire of the authorities? Where is the Pope?"

I scanned the room and spotted His Eminence seated off to my left, fanning his tongue with his zucchetto, having just sampled a fiery mouthful of Ethiopian sik sik wat for the first time.

"Admit it, Father. The rabbi couldn't have spoken so eloquently without a spot of cake in his stomach, eh? Maybe a slice of pumpernickel?

"I digress. When the time has arrived for speeches, which, at occasions such as these, cannot, and certainly should not, be avoided, I find it necessary to laud those excellent orators and storytellers who have come before me, in whose company I hesitate to place myself. A Munchausen is nothing if not modest. Pericles, Demosthenes, Henley, Twain, to name only a few. Masters all at the turning of a phrase, whose sprinkling words have brought so many flowering metaphors to bloom. But I am neither poet nor politician, and I have never thought my words to carry much weight other than the burden of fact, which, depending on where I stand, could be as light as a boulder or as heavy as a feather. I can see by the looks on your faces that some of you get my meaning, while others do not. That is how it should be. After all, of what use would Munchausen be if he could be read as easily as the books written of him, eh?

"But allow me to slowly sink into the inviting waters of your hospitality and say simply that never have I traveled such a distance only to be greeted with a warmer reception. At times like these, I feel as though I am the sea-weary sailor drawn to the alluring melody of your siren's song, doomed to perish upon the rocks of your love, yet unable to change my course all the same. For I, too, have always much preferred to cruise the warm seas of glorious admiration than aimlessly drift the ponds of obscurity. But rest assured, I have no intention of foundering on the craggy reefs of your recognition. I shall be as that old salt Odysseus lashed to his mast. It is widely known that humility runs in the blood of every Munchausen like green eyes in the Irish. I am no exception. Let it never be said a Munchausen received an ounce of praise without first himself offering a kind word. This gathering is proof enough of your affections, and for that, I am eternally grateful. And now that I have offered my kind word, you are free to heap upon me all the praise you wish without fear of offending my sense of pride."

The assemblage rose as one to its feet and displayed its appreciation through a lengthy applause. Only after some time did the din of the ovation die down. Finally, when quiet was restored was I able to resume.

"I was just speaking with our gracious host, the honorable president here, about the remarkable progress his country has seen these last two hundred years. As many of you surely know, this is not my first sojourn on the American continent. But I need not recall again the details of that harrowing experience tonight. Needless to say, I was all too glad to only lose my scalp and not my entire head in the proposition. When last I was here, this country was an untamed land, populated with natives to whom the notion of freedom was as foreign as a palm tree is to an Eskimo. But the Founding Fathers, for whom life, liberty, and the pursuit of happiness meant so much that they were willing to thrust freedom upon the wild peoples of this land by the barrel of a musket, saw in the promise of this new country a bright future. Winning their own hard-fought battle for freedom, wrenched from the grip of their imperialist masters, set in motion the great democratic experiment the world enjoys to this very day.

"Who among you at this estimable gathering has not himself felt the invigorating buckshot of democracy pierce the windows of his home or his heart, or hasn't spent his last pennies in the wondrous stalls of the free market? Whose tiny voice has not been heard through the megaphone of suffrage, eh? Has it not been to the greater cause of universal human good that the dust of thousands of years of tradition and stolid religions, having done so little to advance civilization, be swept clean by the liberating broom of Western culture?

"If you would indulge me a question further: What need is there even for Munchausen in a democratic society? I must admit, I dwelled on this problem for some time to no resolution. I have come to you, ladies and gentlemen, because I was summoned, and

I see it no less than a moral duty to lend aid where I am able. It is for you and your people to illuminate the way for me. Though the foundations of this glorious American land stand solid on the bedrock of rationalism, I shall ever endeavor to seek out the irrational, which is a natural inclination of mine, and turn its machinations to more sound purposes. All for the glory of democracy, eh? And now a topping off of my scotch, if you please. I never drink wine at gatherings such as these, you know, for as Pliny so pithily put it, there is truth in wine, and a state dinner is hardly the place for the truth, now, is it?"

A second protracted applause brought the crowd again to its feet. After regaining my seat and partaking of a modest portion of Reblochon with fig, a procession of the assemblage ferried past bearing gifts for my journey. From the president of the Swiss confederation came a pair of stout alpine boots; from the emir of Qatar, a grand dhow complete with a crew complement of thirty-five able-bodied sailors. The delegation from Peru presented me a positively exquisite ocarina carved from jaguar bone they claimed was more than seven thousand years old and possessed the mystical power to call forth a demon when played in C minor, or an alpaca when played in C sharp.

The Americans were more modest in their offering, arranging for me a mobile phone, unlimited data usage, of course, which I could use to document my experiences on various social media platforms. This tool, above all others, I have found imminently useful.

Baron@bvonmunchausen · 57min

When last I visited the American continent, it was but a wild, undisciplined, wholly savage land. I see now time and careful refinement has allowed its custodians to cultivate a much more sophisticated savagery.

#fishinabarrel

CHAPTER VI

I remained in the city for several days, always in the company of one or more heads of state, their attics filled with only the most glowing appraisals of the lands over which they held sway. But even an old soldier can have too much flag-waving and jingoism. Soon, my own belfry was ringing with the peals of so many hearty hails and hosannas that to silence the din, I found it necessary to evacuate the capital forthwith and set about on my peregrination of the nation.

Departing just before first light so as to avoid any further celebratory encumbrance, I pointed my feet west and let them wander according to their own desires. In short order, I was a good distance from the city and approaching a sleepy hamlet on the far side of the Appalachians.

As you well know, my one and only other singular pleasure, after traveling, of course, has always been the enjoyment of a good hunt, and it turned out that, while taking a brief respite from the road, I was afforded the opportunity to indulge my venatic avocation.

Before my departure from Washington, an invitation had reached me from one of your captains of industry. A retired marine who, since returning from the field of combat, had founded his own arms company some decades ago. He offered to accompany me to his favorite hunting grounds if I would first oblige him and tour his state-of-the-art manufacturing facilities. Not one to shun the chance to swap tales of battlefield glory with a fellow soldier, I happily accepted.

His factory represented a marvelous marriage of ingenuity and efficiency. No shorter than four dozen football fields, and employing a battery of fascinating apparatus that all but made the necessity of human workers obsolete, the place, I learned, churned out an array of carbines at the impressive rate of five thousand every day. I could only imagine how much more swiftly I could have brought our campaign against the Turks to end had I such arms at my disposal.

The tour concluded, we retired to his private office, a room bedecked in flags, posters, and all manner of trinkets celebrating America and the Constitution. A burly caricature of Uncle Sam hung beside the door, while a plaintive Christ looked on from a spot high above the desk.

Amid this prideful menagerie, we toasted his success over a dram of bourbon, and I heartily thanked him for the opportunity to take a private look, behind the scenes, as it were, at the manufacturing of America's military prowess.

"Oh, these weapons aren't for the army," he quickly corrected me. "The government contracts for that kind of thing. And contracts, as you know, mean paperwork. And paperwork means lawyers, obligations, regulations. All of that impedes business, slows down the process, delays delivery of the product. Smacks of overreach to me. Besides, our guns are much too reliable for military use. It's critically important to my customers that they maintain a competitive edge. Focus groups have shown this time and again. They need to protect themselves, be one step ahead of Big Brother, you know? Hell, it's their God-given constitutional right. No, our rifles are for the home and hearth only. Hunting and home defense. We manufacture solely for the general consumer, the working man, and his family.

All American materials assembled by Americans for Americans. I don't need to tell you, legislatures across the country agree. In most states, you can legally carry one of these puppies even before you're old enough to vote. What's more free than that? And I can assure you our streets have never been safer because of it. I take enormous pride in my product, sir. But why take just my word for it? How about giving one a spin?"

I must admit, it was a tempting offer. Though I have always been a fierce advocate of superior firepower when settling matters of warring nations, I hold firm to the belief that in hunting game, a province of the gentleman, one's arms should be comparable only to the task undertaken. To bag a single unarmed beast in the wild, a single well-placed shot is all that is required, if the hunter be skilled enough. I have never needed anything more, so I politely declined his offer, and instead charged my musket with a single ball, and the two of us proceeded as friends to a local wood to pursue our leisure.

Not long after setting off into the underbrush, we became temporarily separated, he being more familiar with the terrain than me, and I was left to navigate alone.

For nearly an hour, I neither saw nor heard any game larger than a squirrel, and I was beginning to despair that my expedition would prove unfruitful when I caught sight of a broad glade ahead. At the far side stood several small whitetails, females all, and beyond them, watching over his harem, stood a monstrous buck, tall as a Clydesdale and crowned with a veritable briar patch of antlers. I counted no fewer than three hundred points spread five feet on either side of him. To have him as a prize was without question. With only one shot available, I could little afford to risk a miss from so great a distance, but neither could I venture trying to get much closer, as surely so many skittish ears would be easily alerted to my presence and the whole lot would bolt before I could even take aim. So, steadying myself where I stood, I leveled my piece and let fly. The rapport of the blast sent the lot of them to flight, the buck included. My ball, having struck the regal beast squarely between

the eyes from 150 yards, merely glanced off his skull, which was no doubt thick as granite.

Quickly recharging my piece with a fresh ball and double the regular load of powder, I took off in pursuit of my fleeing quarry through the dense scrub. My tenacity paid off, and presently, I emerged from the tangle of brush at the edge of a wide sporting field lined with bleachers opposite which stood a school. Sighting my prize bounding across the pitch at full gallop toward the building, I raced after as fast as my boots would carry me. As I approached the fifty-yard line, I witnessed flocks of children and teachers already scrambling out the exit doors with equal urgency like rats fleeing a sinking ship. No doubt the sight of the huge, frothing buck careening uncontrollably toward them was enough to send them running in terror. Their shouts of panic only served to startle and confuse the monster all the more, so much so that, against all its natural instincts, it ran straight through an open doorway and into the school.

Like a salmon battling its way upstream, so, too, did I force my way against the opposing current of screaming bodies until I gained the threshold.

No sooner had I entered the structure than the whimpers from those still trapped inside with the raging beast met my ears. Several youths, rightly frightened out of their wits, paralyzed with fear, hid under their desks, barricaded behind classroom doors.

"There is no need to panic," I reassured them. "This will all be over presently. Which way did he go?" A little girl's trembling finger directed my step farther down the hall.

Somewhere nearby, a door slammed, followed by a stifled cry. I paused to listen for hoof falls. Suddenly, several shots rang out in rapid succession. Quickening my pace, afeared someone else had designs on bagging my prize, I rounded a corner, and there was the creature, frozen with fright in the very center of the passageway, its massive bulk towering over a group of cowering bodies huddled against a row of lockers.

It is rare that a hunter should get a second bite at the apple, so to speak, so with the beast now cornered, I'd no intention of letting him escape or terrorize the children any further. He rounded his giant head back on me with unbridled rage in his eyes, white froth dripping from the corners of his seething mouth. I spied the bare patch of fur between his eyes from my first shot. Taking aim at this spot, I shouldered my piece and prepared to fire when the sudden materialization of a second hunter threw my whole operation into disarray.

A sulky youth, oddly attired in terribly ineffective camouflage, appeared opposite my position at the far end of the hall, such that the buck now stood squarely between us. Upon sighting myself with my firearm already leveled, the impetuous boy must have thought himself the superior hunter, for he, too, shouldered his weapon, which I recognized as a specimen off the line from my recent factory tour. Equipped with an optical scope and overlarge magazine, he clearly outmatched me in armament. Without warning, and with neither the art of a marksman nor any concern for the innocent children all around us, he let loose a wild barrage of fire, raising cries of terror from all corners of the building.

I hear you gasp. You say to yourself, surely this must be the end of Munchausen? Honestly, you would not be wrong in thinking so, and even I must admit, in the heat of the moment, I considered saying my last prayers. But whereas Lady Fortuna favors the bold, Saint Nemo* prefers to hedge his bets.

I stood my ground and watched as all one hundred or so rounds this troubled fool let fly flew directly into the massive tangle of antlers atop the buck's head, ricocheting about the points like so

---

* Author's note: I felt compelled to stop the baron once again, stating that, though I knew woefully little about Catholic doctrine, I could name more than a few of the saints. And Nemo was a name I was quite unfamiliar with.

"This is not surprising," he said. "He's nobody in particular. I first came across him while perusing a volume of Rodolfus Glaber. An unremarkable life, however, a most useful patron to have when facing insurmountable odds. After all, what any man cannot do, surely *no body* can."

many fish trapped in a barrel, building both tremendous speed and heat until the lot smashed together into a single mass of molten lead big as a thirty-six-pound shell. It soon reached a critical state, and with nowhere else to go, the huge ball released all its pent-up energy and rocketed straight up through the ceiling, leaving a hole ten feet across in its wake. Describing a wide arc across the clear blue sky, it did not come down again for nearly a mile.

This sudden turn of events threatened to send my buck into a fresh panic, and thinking him ready to bolt again, I seized my opportunity and quickly fired. This time, my overcharged shot rang true, and my ball flung straight into his open, frothing mouth and passed down his throat and through his gullet and intestines before exiting that part of his fundament that requires no further classification and, clear out the other side, lodging in the breech of the youth's weapon, killing the beast outright while simultaneously disarming my competition in the process.

My quarry now quite dead, I happily removed his prized antlers, from which I later fashioned numerous knife and cane handles I intended to present as gifts at the lunar court. I then took an opportunity to educate the local authorities on the dangers of permitting one barely out his bloom to possess such an unorthodox weapon, one clearly unsuited to the simple task of game hunting. They thanked me for my assistance and agreed to take my suggestions under advisement.

Sadly, my story does not have the wholly happy ending I had hoped for. My companion on the hunt, the owner of that marvelous weapons factory, who had survived three tours on the battlefield, I later learned was killed during our expedition, struck on the head by the massive ball of falling ammunition. I can only take some comfort in knowing he would have been happy it was an American-made rifle, and not some inferior foreign imitation, that ultimately did him in.

"You'll forgive me, Baron, if I detect a thread of karmic whimsy in the weaving of your tales?"

A wistful grin played on his lips. The herring had arrived as ordered, and he'd already dug in with gusto.

"Balderdash," he said, punctuating the point with a jab of his dripping fork. "Karma implies a grander design: just punishments and just rewards. I can assure you there is no such plan to be had. The universe is guided by laws firmly rooted in science, not philosophy."

"And yet you purport the irrational as the foundation of your very being. How can someone like you possibly find footing in the tenets of the scientific method?"

"I don't," he said matter-of-factly. "I make no illusions that mine is a mind of a decidedly unscientific bent. Logic and rationality being the foundations of the so-called scientific method, much as the proton and neutron are the foundation of the atom, irrationality, to which I have dedicated the thrust of my life, and which might be best described as my *raison d'être*, finds little purchase in scientific pursuits. Irrationality is viewed by no small number as very much the antagonist to the protagonist of theory, hypothesis, and method. And rightly so too."

The baron paused to take in another delicate forkful of kipper. I was astonished a dive like the Mare's End would even offer it on its menu. Then again, where the baron was involved, nothing was ever out of bounds. He dabbed the corners of his mouth with a triangle of napkin and continued.

"Nevertheless, I have and always will consider myself a man of science. For it is in the nature of every man to seek out that truth to which he can cleave with all his being, be it one of science or spirit. To each their own, I have always said. Which is why I should now like to relate an extraordinary encounter from my recent travels, one in which I was forced to use science to disprove the very existence of a fellow human being."

"A most improbable feat," I said, baiting the old crank. "Even for you."

"And yet still you will believe it is so," he confirmed, peering over the bridge of his obscenely bony nose. "If you are as much a man of science as I, you have no choice but to believe.

"There is a peculiar anemonefish native to the warm waters of the southern seas possessed of the remarkable ability to metamorphose from male into female when it suits the needs of its community. To be sure, there are other creatures capable of this mode of transmogrification—eels, amphibians, and the like—who have been known to alter their nature in response to their environment. I have even borne witness once to an Indian rhinoceros commuting itself into a house cat to fool a poacher pursuing its ivory. (A tale for another time, perhaps?) But never before had I observed this behavior in the human animal, whose construction, either by God's own hand or some other evolutionary atavistic function, clearly does not allow for it to occur naturally.

"Thus, it was to my utter stupefaction that I should encounter just such an individual possessed of this ability on my travels. The city in which I made their acquaintance is immaterial to my tale, as I have since met many more of the same ilk in various places throughout the country. I have even learned this phenomenon is not bound to just America. Across the globe, other lands are able to boast of their own growing populations. Some of these noteworthy people have even achieved celebrity and higher office, though it could be said by pursuing positions in the ignominious venues of politics and Hollywood, they willingly and irreparably tarnish their own images. I have always said no self-respecting gentleman, or woman, engages in the vulgar pursuit of fame for him or herself alone but rather solely for the glory of king and country.

"In any case, this fellow held to the line that nature had enshrined his spirit in a body of the wrong type. He'd been born a man, you see, yet never quite felt that the right thing. In time, he applied himself to correcting what he viewed as this egregiously cruel error and began living as a woman instead, with some success. However, after a period, this, too, felt wrong for them. By this time, this individual had scorned all conventional forms of address, opting instead to insist, since they fit into neither customary category, they must then naturally be neither.

"I have since observed this paradox taking root mostly in the younger generation, though it is hardly confined to them alone. The individual in question here was no more than sixteen at the time these sensations arose in them."

"It's more and more commonplace these days," I observed.

"And not the least bit preposterous, I might add," the baron added.

"The labeling is proving to be a particular pain point. Endless problems there. The language really doesn't allow for it. Ambiguity is not really humanity's strong suit."

"Which is exactly what I brought to their attention," the baron continued. "I have been around a long time and traversed a great many miles within the confines of our universe. And while I have seen things both wondrous and mystifying, there have been a few constants that are undeniable. Principle among these being the binary nature of the universe. There is up, and there is down. There is yes, and there is no. A thing either is, or it isn't. And if it is not *is*, then it *is not*. And, therefore, it does not exist."

"What about your anemone fish? They freely change form. You just said so yourself," I said, more than a little turned around by these grammatical meanderings.

"Ah, but the change is finite in nature. Once complete, male is female and vice versa. The in-between is but a transition to a final stage. Nothing can be said to truly exist there."

"I'm afraid I don't follow."

"Neither did this person. I say person because, frankly, the fluid nature of their fancy imposed such confusion as to render any other reliable means of identification moot. And neither do most. However, there have been others who understood this concept much better. Take Schrödinger, for example. You are familiar with his famous feline?"

"I am."

"Excellent! As you know, if the cat is locked in a box that one can neither see into, hear into, smell into, nor otherwise access, then there is no way to know if the cat is alive or dead at any given point in time, correct?"

"That's the gist of it," I said. "The very act of opening the box influences the outcome, essentially negating the experiment entirely."

"Precisely. So, if that is the case, and one cannot ever know if the cat is alive or dead, can it be said, then, to even exist at all? You see my point? In a binary universe, a thing either is or isn't. There is no third option. In this case, alive or dead is *only one of the two options*. Alive or dead, the thing itself still exists. But once it is shut away from all conventional means of identification, it becomes nothing at all. A *non-thing*, if you will, removed from existence entirely. Such was the situation of this unfortunate individual."

"But they still exist," I countered. "We can still see them, hear them, touch them."

"A mere grammatical fallacy," the baron said dismissively. "In a binary universe, if I cease to be I, then I become *not I*, therefore I cease to be. Just as this person ceased to be either *he* or *she*. If neither he nor she, then what? There is no third option. Therefore nonexistence. It's simple linguistics. Or maybe it's rhetoric?"

"Your argument is specious at best," I said, "and many would agree not the least bit transphobic."

"Yet another grammatical fallacy. Phobic is fearful. There is nothing to fear from this person's beliefs. I was merely pointing out, scientifically, I might add, that to deny the binary nature of the universe is akin to self-negation. And if someone is going to deny their own existence, why shouldn't I?"

"That's lunacy," I shouted, losing all sense of decorum. "Using words to deny a person's very humanity. It's fascism, that's what it is. It doesn't sound at all like the baron I know. It borders on nihilism. I can't believe you would even say such a thing?"

My rising ire was quickly quelled by a sudden burst of laughter from the baron.

"Ho-ho!" He rocked in his seat. "Had you there, did I? I do so love a good verbal joust every now and again. Top marks for holding your ground."

I took a sip of wine to help regain my composure.

"So, you don't really believe any of that?"

"Deny someone's existence through pure semantics? Of course not. That would be a feat, even for me. No, I was merely pointing out one of the verbal traps I've heard so many fall into before. This one says they're not a he or a she, that one insists that they are. Some focus so much on their own struggles they forget the struggles of others. Then comes the shouting, the abuse, the rage, on both sides. Words, all just words. As someone who lives and dies on the page, I know a little something about words too, you know. Take out *he* and *she*, and what are you left with? Just a jumbled mass of dialogue where no one hears anything, no one listens to anyone else, everyone talks over each other, and no one character can be clearly identified. Now, who'd want to read a story like that?"

CHAPTER VII

It may astonish you to know there have been a few times in the last three hundred years when it would have been better to not be Baron von Munchausen. I know, I know, you must think me mad. How could it possibly be that anyone would want to be anything other than the person they were born to be, let alone a person so illustrious as Munchausen? Yet I can assure you, circumstances have dictated it be so on more than one occasion. Shall I tell you of just one such time?

I have previously related to you the close call I had with the emir of Kokand, but that was not the only episode where I became the unfortunate victim of unlucky timing. I remember being called to the home of a certain minister to the throne of Napoleon III. The year was 1853, and His Highness was then engaged in preparations for an expedition to Crimea to join the British and the Turks in repelling the unwanted advances of the tsar.

It was the hope of this minister, who was in the service of the emperor as a close counselor of war, for me to accept a field commission and lead the French into battle, and to that end, he organized a dinner in my honor where he believed the presence of several generals and their wives would prove sufficient persuasion for me to take up the mantle of *général de l'armée* in the service of His Majesty and the republic.

Having decided I could do no less than accept the honor, I proceeded to his home on the banks of the Seine to inform him of my decision. This was in the early afternoon, and it was my intention to have a private meeting where we could hash out the details of my appointment before a formal announcement was made later that evening at the dinner. But when I arrived, I found my host and his retinue had been called out on official business, his home thus being occupied by only the servants and his lovely daughter, Sara, a girl of nineteen, and already possessing many of those qualities distinguishing her sex as the fairer. Beautiful, kind, and known to display both modesty and fire in equal measure, after an hour's conversation in the parlor, this delicate creature had quite quickly fallen in love with me, and I with her. Presently we found ourselves in the garden lost in the entanglement of an amorous embrace. This bliss, which carried away with it all sense of time, was broken only by the chatter of the minister returning with his retinue, among whom I neglected to add was a certain handsome lieutenant, the young Sara's affianced. The situation seemed dire. Trapped outdoors with no place to hide, knowing if I were discovered that not only my commission but my very life would be forfeit, for the offense of love's dishonor could only be answered in the form of a duel, I was forced to employ extreme measures to conceal our tryst. Availing myself of a few drops of tincture I acquired once while touring the Aegean coast near Thessaloniki, sold to me by a traveling merchant and said to be distilled from the same waters of the spring in Halicarnassus, where the ill-fated lake nymph Salmacis and the poor Hermaphroditus were coalesced into one, I was instantly transformed from a man into a beautiful woman.

I had little time, though, to glory at the radiance of my own newfound femininity, for just as the potion's effects crystalized, we were beset by the minister and his entourage. Sara introduced me as her friend Carmina, and we were both thoroughly showered with compliments by all the men present, including Sara's fiancé, who took a particular fancy to me, offering to hold my hand and recite a few lines of poetry to boot, all the while completely ignorant of the fact he was making love to his rival. Interpreting my coquettishness as enticement for further advances, the fool made little mystery of his feelings for me. The fanning of his amorous flames served only to incense the jealousy of Sara, who, in a fit of puerile envy, revealed my true identity and the means of my transformation. Suffice it to say, I took flight, narrowly escaping with my life and honor intact, and only the siege of Sevastopol the worse off for my absence, for had my commission come through, we would have surely taken the city in a matter of hours.

After departing the Appalachian foothills, I passed through a town whose inhabitants were themselves in the midst of a considerable transformation as well. Though my own metamorphosis was born of necessity, these folks willingly sought to transubstantiate for no other reason than pure caprice. A sort of fervor had seized them, and not content with merely exchanging genders, they altered themselves in a variety of ways, each according to his or her own fancy.

There remained not one citizen in this town, young or old, male or female, who had taken it into their head to remain as their creator had made them. Indeed, there were few who could still be considered part of the human species at all, such was the extremity of their transformations. They had become cats, rabbits, shrubs, walking sticks, ceiling fans, and rubber stamps. The town postmaster had thought tobecome a clock, and had his arms surgically removed and replaced with a pair of long metal spades, the right slightly longer than the left. People came from far and wide every day to watch as he stood atop the pediment of city hall and struck twelve, proudly bellowing out the Westminster Quarters, neither snow nor rain nor heat nor gloom of night staying his timekeeping duties. A

beautiful socialite, a woman of some standing in the community, I was told, had recently become a rose garden with thorny blooms sprouting from her every orifice. At first sight, I became concerned for her physical health. Happily, my fears were quickly assuaged. I was informed she was watered daily and pruned twice yearly.

Children were not immune from this transformative craze, the whimsy of their parents giving rise to a surplus of pint-size construction vehicles, stuffed bears, dinosaurs, and dollhouses. One child's desire to become as strong as the heroes he'd seen in the motion pictures had prompted the implant of more than sixty pounds of muscle tissue in his arms and torso, while another, who had expressed a curiosity about the lives of fish, had her lungs replaced with gills and was living in a nearby lake.

I inquired the mayor of this town—who was himself midway through his own transition to become a pickup truck, his legs having already been amputated and substituted with a set of steel-belted radial tires—if anyone ever expressed regret about having undergone their changes, particularly the younger generation. I related my own metamorphic experience with the minister of war's daughter, and that while it had lasted only a few hours, it still left no lingering doubt the man I had been born was certainly the same one I should be when I ultimately meet my end. He sympathized and admitted there were times when some regretted their choices.

"Mistakes have been made from time to time," he said, and introduced me to his own daughter, who at the age of just eight felt in the depths of her soul she should have been born a duck, owing to her joint affinity for both swimming and flight. This girl's wish was granted, and though the process was laborious and quite painful, she succeeded in her dream and lived quite happily for several months as a large rosy billed pochard. That was, until winter came, and she was forced with the others in her flock to migrate south. It was true her transformation had been complete, but given her overlarge size, extended periods of flight proved dreadfully taxing, and on more than one occasion, she simply dropped out of the sky like a stone from exhaustion. Faced with the prospect of having to perform these labors twice yearly, along with constantly having to be on guard against foxes, snapping turtles, and the occasional spray from a hunting rifle, the life of a duck rightly proved too overwhelming, and she expressed a desire to return to her feminine form. Sadly, the reversal process was less of a success, and though the regular administration of hormones restored much of her humanity, some ten years on, she continues to mourn the shallowness of men, who find a bill and webbed feet cause to look elsewhere for suitable marriage material.

Baron@bvonmunchausen - 45min

In America, everyone is free to practice whatever religion they so choose. This right is enshrined in the First Amendment. As in everything else, practice makes perfect. Sadly, the Americans have pretty much given up on that part.

#John8:7

CHAPTER VIII

It would be impossible for me to recount for you here all the times I have found myself in unfortunate danger of losing my life. Risking one's skin on the field of battle for honor and glory is a common occurrence in the career of a soldier, and I have had the privilege on many occasions, not a few of which have been recorded in the numerous volumes of my adventures that have pursued me throughout the years, to hazard my life in the arena of war. But not every hair on my neck has been threatened in the meritorious pursuit of battle. Sometimes the most innocent of leisure excursions can be fraught with unanticipated peril. As it happens, Death is not as discerning as a sommelier, and his choice of souls to reap is often apropos of its effect on the dinner service. Fortunately for me, each time he has approached the table, he has found Munchausen's chair vacant, its occupant out for a smoke.

One such episode, which threatened to derail my entire American expedition, occurred while I was visiting the wide-open spaces of the state of Oklahoma. The weather that morning showed promise of bright, clear skies. I set off early on foot with no other intent than drinking in the scenery.

Letting nothing more than chance be my guide, I'd spent several pleasant hours meandering endless fields of wheat when the midday sun's oppressive heat forced me to seek shelter. Scanning the treeless horizon, I spied a barn some two miles away standing prominently against the blanched sky and made smartly for it. It was in a shabby state, but solidly built, and fit to purpose, for I found immediate relief under the shade of its rickety timbers. At first, I thought it abandoned; however, a quick survey revealed I was not its only inhabitant. Standing tied to one of the beams was the gaunt figure of an old, mangy jackass. Whosoever should have placed the poor beast thusly surely had evil in his heart, for there being no farmhouse for miles in any direction, it was clear their intent was to leave the creature to starve. I took pity, brushed away the gnats swarming at his rump, and proffered a few apples I had brought in my pocket for a snack, which he took readily from my hand and munched with the stoic reserve animals of his ilk are renowned for. Finding I had no additional food to give, my companion remained standing where he was, regarding me impassively, while, for my part, still exhausted from the morning's walk, I took to an old plank bench and lay down for a brief nap.

I might have slept there the whole of the afternoon were I not awoken by the terrible roar of a storm rolling across the landscape. I was rushing to secure the open barn door when I spotted a colossal funnel four miles wide and black as the charred end of the devil's tail descending from the clouds. Tornados are not an uncommon occurrence in those parts, but this one, by far, put all its predecessors to shame with both its sheer immensity and intensity. In a matter of seconds, it passed directly overhead, sweeping up the entire barn and sucking it, me, and my equine companion some ten miles straight into the air.

Thinking myself secure so long as I remained within the structure, I sat down on my bench, lit my pipe, and elected to wait out the storm. Sadly, it soon became apparent that the old, tired lumber would not hold up. Planks tore free from the walls and flung off into the swirling vortex, letting in a fierce wind and needling rain that stung the face like swan shot. Seeing now a need to find more suitable quarters, I was about to take my leave when I recalled the ass, who, through the whole ordeal, had remained standing beside his post, obstinately indifferent to his precarious situation.

By this time, circumstances had become dire. More and more planks and shingles tore free and hurtled off out of sight. Sensing the imminent destruction of our temporary shelter, even the ass began to look worried. I wasted no time. Untying his fetters, I mounted his back and, with a gentle kick from my boot, coaxed him out into the raging torrent. The going was surprisingly easy, the tornado having lifted several large chunks of earth into its swirling mass as it progressed across the land. So as it was, my companion and I had but to walk to the edge of our slab and wait, much like one does on a train platform, until the next clod came passing by.

"Next train, the five o' two to Munich, with stops in Heidenheim, Donauworth, Augsburg, and Landsberg am Lech," I mused to myself to pass the minutes. "Mind the gap."

Presently, a hunk of earth drifted by, and I urged my mount to get on board. Leaping thusly, we were able to descend about a mile through the clouds, my additional weight and the weight of my ass causing each successive mass of soil to sink slowly back toward the ground. I would gladly have continued in this fashion all the way back down to terra firma had I not become distracted by the curiously sonorous harmony of a choir penetrating the rush of the whirlwind. Glancing about, I discovered the source of the singing: upon a passing clod of earth stood a whitewashed church that, like my barn, had been sucked up into the storm.

Two quick leaps landed us firmly at the front door. I tied my mount to a section of fencing, leaving him to graze on a patch of damp grass, and went inside. There, I found the congregation in mid-service, lining the pews, engaged in a chorus of "How Great Thou Art." Not wishing to intrude, I quietly took a seat in the last

row and waited. When they'd finished and retook their seats, the pastor, a chubby little red-faced fellow in a tight suit, paced the crossing before them.

"The Lord Jesus provides shelter for all his children from the storm," he said, eliciting several rousing hosannas from the congregation. "You need but open your heart to Him, and His love will protect you. Do you believe in the righteousness of the Lord Jesus Christ and the commands of His will?"

All present acceded with cries of praise and tears of joy amid the trembling floorboards.

"Excuse me," I said, drawing all eyes to myself. "For my part, I have always entrusted my faith to Saint Nemo, for who better to know God than nobody?"

"All can know the Lord, my friend."

"As can no one," I said. "If *nobody* believes, then he believes for all. Belief in no one is at the very foundation of my creed. And I've no doubt nobody can ride out this storm, yet the peril clearly remains for the rest of us."

"Only sinners who reject the word of the Lord face peril," he replied, raising his Bible high. "And I hear the words of a sinner in your voice, sir, for you claim to believe in nothing, and he who believes in nothing cannot be accepted into the loving arms of Jesus Christ."

"Actually, it's nobody," I corrected. "I know of no Saint Nihil."

He ignored me completely and addressed only his flock.

"You see? It is sinners like this man who have brought this storm upon us. It rages across our country every day, a testament to His wrath for disobedience to His word: sodomites and homosexuals, free to flaunt their perversions in the face of the Lord; women killing the unborn child growing in their womb, God's very gift of life snuffed out without a second thought; Sharia law practiced right here by terrorists in the Lord's chosen country; atheists and Satanists who turn their backs on their one true lord and savior. This storm is a punishment for the sins of this land, sins planted like seeds and allowed to grow into weeds and creep under the very foundations of our great Christian nation. He sent this storm to wash away the stink of the foulness of these sins that offend Him so!"

The members of the congregation showed their appreciation with another spirited round of hallelujahs, but their praise did little to abate the raging torrent, which began to strip the very walls of their sanctuary from around them.

"Then it is safe to assume there are none among you of that sort?" I asked.

"Absolutely not," the pastor said. "This is a house of the Lord's children, who are free of sin and know only His love and mercy."

"I am ever so little the philosopher, sir," I said. "And even less so the ecclesiastic. But as one who deals almost exclusively with the chimerical and, if I may be so humble as to say, is an expert in the unbelievable, I can hardly be faulted by observing your Lord appears more intent on destroying you at this moment than anyone else."

"Jesus protects those who accept and worship Him," he said. "Take Him into your heart, entrust yourself to Him, and you will be saved."

"If it's all the same to you, I'd rather entrust myself to my ass," I replied and, bowing humbly, took my leave. Outside, my mount waited patiently where I'd left him, and together we rode off with ease, catching the next clump of earth to come sailing by. Our timing could not have been more fortuitous, as mere seconds after my departure, the church and its entire assembly were hurled out of the whirlwind with so much violence, they did not come down for some four or five miles distance, only then to be smashed completely to bits against a hillside, bringing all inside to an abrupt and unfortunate end.

The storm raged on for some time, before eventually exhausting itself. Seeing an opportunity to escape, my dutiful companion used his own innate judgment to guide us safely out of the squall and back down onto solid ground. We alighted in a field beside an apple orchard, and as a reward for his courage and cool-headedness, I led him through the gates and allowed him to eat his fill.

CHAPTER IX

I admit to being singularly impressed with the stoic courage and quiet resolve my ass had displayed during the storm, which I could attribute to nothing other than his being of an extraordinary lineage. Creatures of his ilk are notorious for their stubborn sense of self-preservation, which, though it sometimes leads to harsh words and even the odd spiteful rap of a switch across their hind, nonetheless leaves them doggedly unmoved. Which is why my companion's willingness to venture out into such dangerous conditions left me curious as to the origins of his gallantry. Clearly, his breeding had instilled in him an unusual bravery, and having met only one other of his kind with similar fearlessness, I concluded that this ass was none other than a direct descendant of Dapple, the noble beast ridden by Sancho Panza, the humble squire of my good friend Don Quixote de la Mancha!

With this pedigree established, and firm in the knowledge my mount would prove both a loyal and brave companion, as his forebears had no doubt done, the progenitor of his line being especially notable for following his master into countless battles with little hope himself of escaping unscathed, I set out for further adventure.

Nothing important of note occurred for the next several days, and both Pinto and I were free to take our leisure undisturbed where we may. I'd dubbed him Pinto because of his pie-bald coat, which, much like his forefathers', returned full and healthy after some decent feedings and a little sunlight.

We became fast friends. Pinto proved an excellent listener and a fastidious navigator. His innate sense of direction leading us steadily over hill and dale, only occasionally punctuated by periods of steadfast pauses. One of these occurred outside of Las Cruces, New Mexico, where he stood transfixed, observing a low rock wall for nearly seventeen straight hours. Thinking he spied some danger I could not see, I was reminded of the story of Balaam and his ass and thought better than to force the issue. Instead, I used these episodes of waking catatonia best to my advantage, journaling, hunting, and sending out my little observations to the masses through myriad social media outlets.

Eventually, our meanderings brought us to the small village of Haven, a most specious name for such an idyllic little hamlet. For upon reaching the main street, I discovered all the inhabitants, down to the last man, were engaged in the monumental project of erecting a wall around the perimeter of their town. Using whatever was to hand, old fence posts, traffic cones, cinder blocks, discarded appliances, automobiles, and the like, the citizens of Haven worked tirelessly day and night to protect their homes from the barbarians at their gates. When I inquired of some of the residents as to who these invaders were, having passed no artillery positions, brigades, or other signs of a hostile military presence on my way in, I was directed to a small encampment to the west of town.

The mere mention of that place sent most of the citizens to flight. Some, so incensed at the thought of their town being overrun, redoubled their efforts at the wall, while others locked themselves in their homes or places of business, looking to secure their valuables and livelihoods. Amid the chaos, I made my way to the town hall, where six aldermen sat drafting a communiqué directed to the governor begging for more resources and manpower to push back the intruders. My arrival at this most perilous time was met with a sigh of relief, as word of my many successes on the battlefield has always preceded me. Now, before these embattled folk stood Munchausen, and surely, he would come to their rescue.

"Gentlemen," I said. "Take heart. What kind of soldier would I be were I to let this town fall? But before I embark on a campaign to eradicate your enemies, I must first be read into the facts of the situation. Now, what is the nature of this army laying siege to your fair town? I see no platoons, no battalions, about."

"They come for our homes!" one councilman cried, his meaty double chin rippling above his sweat-stained collar. "They come for our jobs! Barbarians is what they are."

"They take and take, and give nothing in return," shouted another.

"They bring disease," said a third. "Draining our resources. They bring their young but refuse to teach them our ways, and yet they expect us to respect their ways. It's madness. It's the very definition of irrational."

"I know a little something about the irrational," I said. "You might even say it's my stock in trade. Now, about your wall—"

"Yes, the wall," they said in unison. "The wall's the key. If the government won't help us, we'll help ourselves. A wall to keep them out. It's the simplest solution, really. Will you help us build it?"

"I have seen walls work in the past with some success," I said. "Provided they are constructed in the right way. But barbarians, as you so call them, rarely engage in siege warfare. They usually favor shoot-and-scoot tactics. Are you wholly sure of your enemy's intentions? Have you scouted their positions? Taken stock of their numbers?"

"All of that is irrelevant," the first councilman replied. "They're at our doorstep, and that's all we need to know. We know what they want, and they can't have it. We've got to protect our community, our families. We need a wall, sir. You've got to help us."

A Munchausen's work is never done, as you no doubt have heard the saying go. I agreed to their request for aid. But if necessity is the mother of invention, then knowledge is at least the cousin of innovation. It would do no good to put up fortifications without a clear picture of the besiegers' capabilities. A basic strategy had to be developed before any real work could begin.

Having had some dealings with hooligans and vandals in the past, I felt it prudent to first make a reconnoiter from a safe distance so as to observe the enemy unnoticed. I waited until nightfall to lessen my chances of being detected and rode out on Pinto toward the glow of small fires burning on the horizon.

The invaders had established a rough camp at the edge of a heavily wooded area: tarpaulin strung between trees to created shelter from the sun and rain, and a few ramshackle lean-tos crafted from sheets, blankets, and few meager belongings. Roughly a dozen camping tents pitched just beyond the tree line, nothing more. In total, I counted no more than 150 men, women, and children. Hardly a force to be reckoned with, though I posited more could be stationed deeper in the wood. Even so, finding them more refugee rabble than barbarian horde, I saw little danger at hand. They were completely unarmed, undernourished, and obviously exhausted.

Taking Pinto by the bridle, I boldly strode into the heart of their camp. Some retreated further into their tents at the sight of my approach. Mothers hurriedly gathered their young ones to breast. All followed me warily with their eyes. For my part, I wore a smile, waved hello, and tried my best to allay any fear or suspicion of my intentions. A profound hush fell over the camp. The only sound to be heard was the crackling of flames from the small campfires burning all about.

Before long, five or six men designated to represent the group stepped forward to parley. These fellows, in the tradition of the hospitality of their homelands, offered me a little food and ale from their meager stocks, which, despite my repeated objections, they would not allow me to refuse. In exchange, I procured from my sack slung across Pinto's back a quantity of Yrdlspretz, a soft green cheese harvested from the milk of the lunar camel, which, in addition to being sweet and delicious, has the added benefit of temporarily lending its eater a bright, iridescent glow. This, as several of the camp mothers soon discovered, can make keeping tabs on small children at night a much easier task.

After cigarettes were passed around and strong coffee gulped down, the immediate matters at hand were raised for discussion. To facilitate our summit, I adopted my host's native tongue.

"They call us invaders," one man spoke up. "Aliens. We are not these things."

I listened as they each told their stories in turn. Many were fleeing poverty, though a few fled exploitation and indentured servitude. Some robbed or stole to feed themselves and had been labeled criminals. All were looking for work and steady wages.

"Your motives are quite irrelevant to the residents of Haven," I said. "They are determined to keep you out at all costs. It might be best if you moved on."

"There is nowhere else for us," an old woman said. "Wherever we go, it is the same. Can't you help us? Explain to them we only want a chance?"

The pleas of the impoverished have never failed to pull at my heartstrings. What man, irrational or otherwise, could not help be moved by the plight of people just trying to live as everyone else? I could no more turn my back on these folks than I could the people of Haven, who could find no peace at the thought of surrendering their town. Fortunately, in a flash, an equitable resolution presented itself in my mind, and I set about bringing my idea to life.

At first light, I mounted Pinto and headed back into town, directly for city hall. The aldermen, eager to hear report of my reconnoiter, pressed me on all sides for details of how I had vanquished their enemy single-handedly.

"It is my sad duty to inform you your barbarians remain entrenched at the city limits," I said. "But fear not, Munchausen gave his word to help, and so he will. I have now in my possession detailed schematics for a wall of such height and breadth as to secure the residents of this village from any further assault. The wall of Dubrovnik will be as an anthill in comparison. But to accomplish this task, I require funds. Throw open your coffers and go 'round to the citizenry. Tell them Munchausen will rescue them, and their contributions are vital to affect the success of our venture."

Word spread quickly, and in no time at all, I was presented with a pile of cash, which I assured the citizens of the town would be employed for the purpose of securing materials and laborers for the project. I told them to no longer fear for their safety, and so happy were they that all headed to the local community center to arrange a party in my honor.

After this, I rode Pinto back out to the encampment, where construction operations began in earnest. I secured the assistance of fifty able-bodied young men eager for work, to accompany me to a nearby wood. It might have taken a fully outfitted logging crew weeks to clear enough land to supply the lumber for my wall. Fortunately, I was carrying among my things the very ax used by Paul Bunyan during his lumberjack days, which made swift work of the cutting. In just a few hours, I'd felled nearly five thousand acres of forest, the men of the encampment working in teams to trim off excess branches and load the logs on Pinto's back, the obliging beast never even batting an ear at the burden he shouldered. On the contrary, he waited with saintly patience as trunk after trunk was loaded up and he was led off by the bridle back to town, where the logs, some well over one hundred feet long, were secured in place.

The people of the encampment were quite industrious and, unlike their American counterparts, unencumbered by union rules and were happy to put their idle hands to good use. The men toiled alongside me, while the women and elderly prepared refreshments, mended torn shirtsleeves, and removed splinters. In total, all hands, save the youngest children, pitched in, and when the work was done, I presented the group with the monies provided by the citizens of

Haven. By day's end, the colossal fortification was complete. Night had fallen, and we all retired to the camp for a well-earned meal and rest.

At midmorning the following day, we were awoken by screams of terror emanating from behind the wall. The residents of the town, who had been only marginally observing the construction, had spent much of the previous day drinking, dancing, and otherwise celebrating their impending victory over their interlopers. Busy carousing behind the closed doors of the community center, they had failed to take full account of the sheer scale of the project. A Munchausen does not suffer half measures. I gave my word that the wall of Haven would dwarf that of Dubrovnik, and so it did.

Nearly a mile high and one hundred feet thick at the base, the great Haven walls completely encircled the city. To ensure their stability, it was necessary they be built at inward angles so as to prevent them from toppling outward under their own massive bulk. The end result was a structure resembling a large teepee with a three-hundred-foot-wide hole at the top to allow for ventilation. Of course, this also resulted in the almost complete blocking out of the sun, except for a two-hour period each day when it passed directly overhead. But this, I assured the residents, would only occur in the summer months. The rest of the year, they could expect just one hour of sunlight each day, so they should plan accordingly.

"But how are we to live?" they cried out as one from behind the wall. Seeking to maximize security, I'd made no provisions for a gate. "We'll die in here."

"Fear not," I said. "History has shown time and again that sieges rarely last more than a year, maybe two, though the residents of Ceuta did manage to hold out for a full thirty against the Moroccans. No matter, though, I'm sure your enemy will eventually tire out and move on; they almost always do. Good luck to you."

With the town secure, I took my leave. Stopping by the encampment one last time to bid everyone goodbye, one of those from the invading horde said they'd only wished to live in a place where they could be safe and prosper, something they could not do in their own homelands.

"They say the grass is greener on the other side, Baron."

"That may be true elsewhere," I said. "Regrettably, not here. It is the dream of every man to wish it so. But you will have to look further afield for your greener grass, I'm afraid. Beyond that wall, all of it will soon be quite dead."

"I am dismayed you would suggest the presence of a thread in my stories," the baron said. "Theme and allusion are the tools of the author, not the actor. I can imbue my tales with no more meaning than I could put pen to paper and write your book for you. That's the problem with you authors. You never want to take the responsibility for your own ideas. It's so much easier to saddle your characters with your politics."

"That wasn't my intent," I protested.

"Your predecessors said as much too." Munchausen snickered, the crow's-feet at the corners of his wizened eyes grotesquely creeping toward his ears. I could have sworn I caught the hint of a faint crinkling. "Oh, it's all right. You lot can do no better than what you were made to do. I suppose we've all a part to play, don't we? Still, you cannot rightly deny me the point. I am hardly a man of politics, and I've said as much time and again.

"When Krzhizhanovsky got it into his skull to send me off to the Soviet Union, do you think he did so at my behest? I enjoy travel as much as the next man. But Moscow in March? That would hardly have been my first choice. Oh, it was a fascinating expedition, a fact-finding mission, really, if you go in for facts of that sort. What I saw and heard bordered on the unimaginable. But all for a purpose. He saw to it. I would have preferred to take the role of passive observer, documenting all I witnessed for the sake of posterity alone, not to advance his agenda of dissent. Munchausen takes no sides, never has."

"Now, wait a minute," I said. "I read Krzhizhanovsky. You never went to Russia at all. Made the whole thing up. Your lies defeated by sound truth. Nothing you could report was so outrageous as to eclipse the preposterous reality Stalin had created."

"Did I invent the whole thing? To be honest, I can't recall. It's been almost one hundred years, you know. But that doesn't change the fact that you've elected to follow right in his footsteps. I was quite content to spend my twilight years in the enfolding robes of obscurity, not traipsing all over creation yet again just to fulfill another hack's desire to jab their nib between the ribs of authority."

"But we need you," I said. "Now more than ever."

"Yes, you've told me already. Scheerbart needed me too, to expound on the ideals of architectural expressionism or some such nonsense. Another talentless penpusher that had me traveling to planets too distant to even comprehend (and Australia, of all places, to boot!) just so he could lord over his contemporaries how superior he felt his own utopian philosophy of architecture to be. What the hell do I know about glass modernism? What does anybody, really?"

"And what about Rudolf Raspe?" I said. "Without him—"

At the mention of the name, the baron hotly folded his arms across his chest. A contemptuous smirk creased the corner of his mouth as he turned aside. For the second time, I detected an obscure yet distinctly raspy crinkle emanating from his direction.

"A bookish little chiseler," he said. "An interloper, and an appropriator of not only my tales but my very life. Did you know, if not for him, I'd have been dead and buried long ago?"

"You owe your immortality to him, then?"

"*Owe* suggests a debt," he said. "I never borrowed so much as a fig from the man. And I certainly don't recall ever inviting him to dine at my table."

"If not for him, we wouldn't be having this conversation. If not for any of them, the world wouldn't know anything of Munchausen. It's a shame you think your immortality is a kind of curse. To anyone who knows you, it's a blessing. There are statues to your greatness, whole museums, even. They've made movies about you. Hell, the Latvians even put you on a coin once."

At the mention of all this adoration, the tension about his whole face softened. The stern side-eye glare eased, and a joviality returned to his visage. He took a few deliberate puffs of his pipe.

"They do like me, don't they?"

"As do I," I said. "And to be honest, agenda or not, I'm quite honored you'd place me in the same company as Raspe and the others. They wanted nothing more than your help to bring a little light in the dark times. I just want the same."

"I do spin a good yarn, don't I," the baron said contentedly. "Like Theseus and the Minotaur, you can always find your way to daylight if you just follow the string."

CHAPTER X

Having successfully rescued the inhabitants of Haven from certain overrun and noting what further benefits it could provide the American populace at large (who do seem very much to enjoy highlighting their extreme diversity of opinions as somehow strengthening their unity), I set about a campaign of wall building.

When seized with a fervor for projects of an industrial nature, I often find it difficult to stop myself. This was the case, as you well know, when I caused to be erected an immense bridge of stone so as to connect the central region of the African continent, where I was at the time, with England, where urgent business requiring my presence necessitated my return posthaste.

I hear you object. Munchausen, you say, where a bridge connects, a wall divides. How can division be a benefit to anyone in a free society? Shall I tell you just how such a thing came to be?

To observe the effectiveness of my program, one need look no further than California, a state perpetually at odds with itself, owing largely to its vast area. Sociopolitical divisions between the bohemians of the north and hedonists of the south have historically kept any meaningful change from taking root. Ongoing debates about the long-term effects of the dairy and meat industries on the environment in direct conflict with rapidly expanding urbanization. The freewheeling, utopia-driven vision of Silicon Valley gurus against the harsh realities of an ever-growing homeless and jobless blight. The list goes on and on. I could think of no better candidate to test my theory on. If neither region could ascend while shackled to the other's dissent, then physically freeing each from the other could not but resolve the issues for both.

My new rampart, which no less matched in scale and strength the dimension of the Haven construction, was made that much sturdier by the addition of thousands of towering redwood and sequoia trunks procured from both the northern and southern forests of the state, thus ensuring an equal division of material supply.

It began at the border northwest of Las Vegas, tracing a line through Death Valley, cutting between Fresno and Bakersfield, and terminated at the sea just south of the city of Monterey. The only bone of contention between the northern and southern factions being which would retain ownership of the famed golf links at Pebble Beach. Resolving this matter proved far from easy, and completion of construction halted while both sides attempted to hash out a mutually satisfactory arrangement. Representatives from the north offered to cede the Monterey airport in exchange for the course. The south said the north could have Clint Eastwood and the entire town of Carmel-by-the-Sea. Neither would agree to the other's terms. With days turning into weeks, and at a stalemate, I took matters in hand and enacted my own judgment of Solomon, bisecting the land along a path between the fourteenth green and the sixth tee box, thereby creating two nine-hole courses. Now everyone could happily lay claim to the legendary Pebble Beach name while still able to boast of being the home to the world's most famous golf course.

With the wall finished, the governors from both sides invited me to tour their respective states. Newly separated and free of the other's objections and legislative stonewalling, each moved to enact the changes they so eagerly desired.

In the San Francisco Bay area, a movement was well underway to make North California the first state in the union to live entirely vegan, with all dairy and pork farms converted to soybean and cornfields. Overnight, millions of head of livestock were liberated, set free to roam as they pleased, alleviating decades of collective guilt plaguing those who opposed their beastly servitude.

Steps were taken to bring freedom and equality to the animal populace at large as well. Up and down the coastline, commercial fishing vessels were sunk on their moorings, their nets cut apart and sewn into fashionable albeit ill-smelling clothing. Hunting in any form was abolished, and the wildlife, which is abundant in that part of the country, was left unfettered to balance itself according to the natural order of species, with the result that there quickly arose an explosion in the population of elk, bears, bobcat, cougars, and other forest creatures. Wolves, which, up to then, were only known to exist in single numbers, experienced pack growth not seen since pre-Columbian times.

Consequently, humans no longer found themselves at the top of the food chain. In a panic, many towns and cities demanded my wall-building services; only, this time, the barbarians at the gate were not invading families of peripatetic plebeians but hordes of carnivorous beasts skulking about the shrubbery for an opportune lunch. This gave rise to a call for more walls, a cry which became so great, I could no longer keep up, and I petitioned the governor for assistance. A volunteer campaign was enacted with more than three hundred thousand men enlisted to help wall off every city, town, and hamlet, which we were able to accomplish in less than three months and with the loss of only seventeen thousand to the enemy.

Stepping over my wall, I found South California was itself just then in the midst of its own crisis. Fires burning with the intensity of a thousand suns sprung up across the land, forcing people out of house and home, an annual phenomenon I am told not uncommon in that region. Millions had already been driven to the sea to escape the ever-encroaching infernos, and thousands had already drowned for their panic. The governor, at her wits' end, beseeched me to intercede and save her people.

"On my honor, Your Honor," I told her. "A Munchausen never retreats."

Quickly assessing the situation, I contrived a threefold plan, which I enacted directly.

First to be done was the rescuing of the citizens drowning in the sea. This proved little challenge. As you know, the eastern region of South California is comprised almost entirely of desert. This overabundance of sand, usually without value, now showed itself a precious commodity. Recruiting three million men for labor, I had them form single-line bucket brigades stretching from Los Angeles east to the Mojave, and using this system of manual conveyance, I had them transport sand from one end of the state to the other, depositing it into the ocean day and night. Within just a few days, a new isthmus of land had been created, connecting the mainland to the Channel Islands, where the retreating masses could stand safely out of harm's way and no longer trade a burning grave for a watery one.

With the populace temporarily safe, I next turned my attention to the fierce Santa Ana winds feeding the flames. These, I sought to tame using the old adage of fighting fire with fire; only, this time, I would be fighting wind with wind. I advised the governor of my designs, and she willingly provided the manpower. Thousands of wind turbines, each five hundred feet high, all facing east, were built along a line stretching from Mexico to the North California border wall. Spinning day and night, these would repel the incoming winds, thus completely negating their ability to further fan the flames.*

---

* Author's note: I again interrupted the baron to inquire if the rumors were really true, and that this wind wall was a direct cause of the Great Utah Haboob, which claimed nearly twenty-six thousand lives and resulted in the complete destruction of Salt Lake City. Munchausen, always cognizant of his critics, though few and far between as they may be, simply scoffed, and again cited his strict adherence to universal laws, even the one of unintended consequences.

The final portion of my plan, extinguishing the flames themselves, relied on economics rather than manpower. I simply inquired of each homeowner in the state the status of their finances, and finding countless numbers of them underwater on their mortgages, I relieved them of their aqueous burden by collecting the excess water and pouring it on the fires, thereby putting out the inferno while simultaneously rescuing thousands of homeowners from drowning in debt.

CHAPTER XI

As is often the case with creatives, among whose numbers I count myself, where there are ups, there are downs. When one is seized by the rising tide of inspiration, a flurry of activity is sure to follow. But it is in the nature of the tides to ebb, and when the waters of creativity recede back into the vast ocean from whence all genius springs, the heart moves on to other endeavors. With Munchausen, it is no different.

I'd grown weary of my walls, and though demand remained at an all-time high, I retired from that industry when I left the Californias. Standing just outside the city limits of Yuma on my journey back East, I thought it only equitable to give Pinto leave to rest as well. His last burden borne upon his bristly back, I untethered his bridle and set him to wander the dusty scrub at his leisure. No sooner had I gifted my friend his freedom than a shimmering limousine motorcade bearing diplomatic flags emerged on the horizon. They pulled to a halt by the roadside, and I was approached by several emissaries sent by His Majesty, the king of Spain, bearing warm wishes and a request. It seemed word of my trusty mount had reached the ear of the king, who hastily dispatched an entourage to collect Pinto and offer him permanent refuge in his ancestral homeland of La Mancha, where he would be free to live out his days in peace. I admit parting with my trusted companion was difficult, but melancholy does not become a soldier, so I took quiet comfort in the knowledge one day fate might again reunite me with another descendant of his noble line.

Not long after our parting, an unexpected letter reached me by courier. This was early April, and as you may have heard reported, I'd just posted a final round score of fifty-nine at The Masters and was being fitted for a green jacket when my presence was requested at the headquarters of a certain multinational finance corporation in the bustling metropolis of New York City. This organization, as the letter explained, had found itself in dire financial straits, and the board of directors had come to the conclusion that only Munchausen was equipped to save them.

I myself have tangoed with the devil of commercialism from time to time, mostly in the fur exchange, and though I sometimes took a hiding, if you'll excuse the pun, I more often than not came out on top. So, you would not be taken aback to learn that during my stay in America, I added *chief executive officer* to my growing list of titles. I was determined to help in whatever way I could.

The letter also informed me that the corporation's private jet service was standing at the ready to bring me to New York forthwith. Normally, I would have refused, but sensing the urgency of the matter at hand, I elected just this once to avail myself of their offering, and wisely used the time en route to familiarize myself with the company and its business dealings.

When we landed, I was met by a driver and shown to a corporate limousine. He offered a glass of scotch from a decanter concealed behind a small panel in the car's door, which I politely declined. In matters of the heart, and the wallet, a clear head is most valued. In a flash, we were off, whisking through the streets of the Big Apple.

A short time later, we pulled up to our destination: a shimmering fifty-three-story steel-and-glass monument to capitalism in the heart of lower Manhattan. Standing in two columns lining the path from street to door, a bevy of the company's executives waited to welcome me like Caesar returned from Pompey. The head of this group, the sitting chairman of the board of directors, stepped forward with a broad smile and firmly grasped my outstretched hand between his.

"Herr Baron," he said. "You do us a great honor."

"The honor is mine," I replied. "I came as soon as I read your letter. I understand there is some service you look to me to perform?"

"Yessir, that is correct. But you must be exhausted after your flight. How about a little rest and refreshment? It's five to noon, and we've got a standing reservation for a quarter past. Shall we?"

"Shouldn't we get to the matter at hand?" I protested as I was guided back toward the waiting limousine. "Your message suggested the situation was quite dire. We should begin posthaste."

"And we will," he said, his gleaming teeth a pearly wall of impenetrable insistence. "We'll get right down to brass tacks, I promise. But we can hardly conduct business on an empty stomach, can we?"

I could see my objections would shatter like mere crystal when hurled against that ivory wall, so I abandoned my protestations and allowed myself to be shuffled back into the car, while the other executives, twenty-two in all, filed by in twos and threes into a pool of waiting limousines (four men I observed retired back into the building only to reemerge moments later on the roof boarding the company helicopter), and together, this motorcade paraded back through the downtown streets, depositing us at the door to one of the city's finest dining establishments.

At the restaurant, we were graciously led to a large table already set for our party and attended to by a small army of waiting staff. Amid warm mahogany paneling and snow-white linens, our band feasted on grilled snapper, Chilean sea bass, rare strip steaks, and pomme frites dipped in creamy rémoulade. These they washed down with imported mineral water and bottles of merlot or pinot grigio, each to their own tastes.

For my part, I ate but little, contenting myself with simple salad greens and a few slices of buttered bread. When a fresh virgin calf was led in and slaughtered tableside for the saltimbocca, I declined my portion, much to the concern of all present.

"Baron, sir," the chief financial officer said. "You've hardly eaten a thing."

"Quite right," I said. "At my age, all is how it should be. A three-hundred-year-old body requires little coal in the firebox to keep the engine running. Please, don't let me stop you. Tell me, all of this wasn't arranged just for my benefit, was it? I am deeply honored, but you needn't have gone to all this trouble and expense."

A general laugh spread across the table.

"Nonsense," the chair of the board chimed in. "This is our standing Friday business lunch. For your celebration, we've got something much bigger planned, don't you worry."

Waitstaff cleared the table and sopped up the residual blood before serving dessert. Crème brûlée, and flaming bananas Foster, tarts, fruit sorbets, chocolate and vanilla mousses, éclairs, all served à la carte, capped off a meal topping twenty thousand dollars, without tip. A wave of the corporate credit card made quick work of the bill, and with lunch concluded, each man in the retinue sauntered back into their waiting limousine (or helicopter) and was driven (or flown) back to the office to continue the business day.

It was getting on three o'clock by the time we returned. A swift elevator ride whisked us up to a corner conference room on the fiftieth floor, where the vacant seat of the recently dismissed chief executive officer sat waiting to accept Munchausen's directorial derrière.

"Baron," the chairman started when all present had taken their seats. "I'll not mince words with you, sir. We are in a state. This economy, and the current administration in Washington, really, has not been kind to us. Employees are turning over faster than a ten-dollar whore. Popular opinion of the financial sector is at an all-time low. Used to be people just gave us all their money and let us run with it. We made billions, and they were content with five, maybe seven, percent annual returns. Now they're asking questions, doing their own research, keeping their money in *savings*."

He spat this final utterance with vitriol. A disgusted grumbling rippled around the table.

"Our profits last year were just half what they were the year before. Do you realize what that means? We barely had enough funds to keep the SEC off our backs, let alone pay our own annual bonuses. Phillips was going to buy an island next year, but now that's off again. And the commerce secretary still expects *his* cut, so we've had to scale back to just three corporate retreats this year instead of the usual four. Bermuda is out, boys."

Another disgruntled murmur shook the table. When the rumbling subsided, I took the floor.

"Gentlemen," I began. "I reviewed your situation on my way here, and I should like to offer my assistance in any way I can. But first, there are a few minute details I require clarification on before I can implement any program of rehabilitation. Firstly, I must ask, what is it this company does, exactly?"

Eye met eye as each looked about the table to the other to provide an answer to my query. Whispered discussions broke out at random. One fellow pulled out an abacus, while another approached a whiteboard and began sketching a large triangle. Finally, the chief financial officer hushed his colleagues and spoke.

"We are a financial investment and analytical firm," he said. "We leverage bond rates and aggressive-growth funds against annuitization of small- and large-cap-asset back loads. Utilizing benchmark diversification and compound-interest expense ratios, we market crypto asset liquidity with considerations for standard deviations in global ticker trends, including, but not limited to, variable yield annuities, 529s and 563s, as well as ensuring our client's buying power as it relates to interest capitalization and contingent liabilities."

"So, you see, it's really quite simple," the chairman said.

"Quite," I replied. "And your employees? What of them?"

"What about them?"

"From what I can see in these numbers, their pay is sufficient on its face. Still, it's far from what I'd call fair or deserved, considering the sheer volume they are expected to produce."

"Are you suggesting a raise? No, sir, that wouldn't do. Studies have shown time and again that the more you pay a man, the less productive he is. Give him more than he needs, and he becomes complacent, starts to slack off. Late for work one day, skipping meetings the next. An analyst in this firm needs to be incentivized to perform above and beyond each and every day, to put in the hours, to sacrifice. That's how he'll get ahead. He looks to us to set the example of the model ladder climber. Rung by rung, that's the way to get to the top."

"I see," I said. "It is the way you achieved your success, then, is it?"

Again, a subdued chuckle bounced about from man to man.

"Well, my father was already a vice president of the firm when I came on as his assistant," the chairman said. "I was fresh off getting my second MBA from Harvard."

"I was a runner for Bear Stearns," chimed in another. "At least for a little while. When my grandfather passed, I inherited a majority share in his company. Then that got bought up, and then bought again."

One by one, each present related the brief history of their acquired wealth, a veritable Decameron of deceit, happenstance, exploitation, and nepotism. When they were through, we moved on to the subject of the company's finances.

"Those should be of little concern to you," I was told. "As president and CEO, I can assure you, you will be more than fairly compensated for your efforts."

"I can see as much," I said. "Which is one of the items I wished to inquire about. Isn't nineteen million a bit excessive for one man's salary?"

"Don't forget, that doesn't include your contractual safety net. A twelve-million-dollar golden parachute."

"I might have had use for one of those during my recent reentry over Albuquerque. But is all the money really necessary?"

"This country is founded on the principle of honest pay for honest work, sir," the chairman said. "People expect their business leaders to be well compensated. And employees don't just see their compensation as something to strive toward their entire lives. It's also a kind of welcome reassurance. If the executive is healthy, then the company must be in perfect health as well. In their hearts, they want to see their betters living it up. Frankly, they need to."

Nods of agreement all around made it clear my opinion on the matter lay in a minority of one. At this turn, I sought to continue with my questions, but before I had the chance, the chairman declared the meeting adjourned so we all might proceed to the fifty-third floor for the aforementioned celebration of my appointment to the presidency. This I wished to avoid at all costs. Making my profound excuses, I informed all present that the day's labors, weighing heavily on my body and spirit, demanded I retire for the evening so I could return fresh and prepared for my first day of work. Begrudgingly, they acceded to my request, and I was promptly chauffeured to my hotel, comfortable in the knowledge they were determined not to let my absence in any way put a damper on the grand festivities they'd arranged. I hear they had to make a public offering of an additional four million shares just to cover the cost of the catering.

The following morning, I returned to my new office bright and early, resolved to take up the reins of my new position with gusto. I'd spent the previous evening reviewing the books and devising a plan to reverse the corporate course, all according to the laws of irrationality.

Some quick calculations revealed my total compensation in comparison to the average employee of the firm resulted in a discrepancy ratio of 108:1. Add in the compensation packages for the entire executive suite, including the board of directors, and the ratio climbed to 163:1.

Taking that ratio, I divided by the Planck constant, added pi, subtracted forty-two, and, reductio ad absurdum, the solution presented itself. Namely, were I to accumulate all the fabric from the executive suites' golden parachutes, I would have just enough silk to stitch a canvas large enough to rig to the company's office tower and sail it to calmer financial waters. Satisfied with my designs, I brought my scheme directly to the board, which received it with little enthusiasm.

"Preposterous! Absurd! Utter financial ruin!"

"Gentlemen," I said, attempting to bring calm and order. "Did you not place your trust in me to save your company? Then why do you doubt Munchausen at this critical juncture? As you can clearly see, we've already got a favorable wind at our backs."

It was true. I'd taken the liberty to enact my plan before approaching them for their thoughts on the matter and appointed a cheery, unpaid post-graduate intern named Peter boatswain to see us out of port. As a reward for the employees' service to the company, I'd used some of the remaining silk to stitch shimmering golden sailor uniforms for one and all, from the executive assistants all the way down to the boys in the copy room. Newly enfranchised, the entire crew set their sights on brighter financial horizons.

The floor-to-ceiling windows of the fiftieth-floor conference room, now the crow's nest, provided us an excellent view as Coney Island drifted past amidships.

"What have you done?" the chairman cried, seeing nothing before us save open water stretching for miles.

"You were clearly sinking the ship, gentlemen," I said. "Staying the course, which is so frequent a stopgap in your industry, simply won't do any longer. To maintain buoyancy, it has become necessary to take a different tack."

I needn't tell you resistance to this new direction was swift. In a flash, calls were made down to security, demands for my dismissal and immediate removal from the building. But when building security arrived, decked as they were in their new golden uniforms, it was the C-suite who found themselves bound in irons and dragged to the brig.

"This all feels a bit of a stretch, even for you, Baron."

"I daresay one would need to be of quite an open mind to, ahem, fathom the meaning behind my little tale, if you catch my drift." He chuckled, pleased with his little josh. "Let me remind you, every word of it is nothing less than the honest truth. I have always loved the salty air of the open sea. You know once, whilst sailing to Ceylon—"

"Let's not get too far off course," I interrupted. "One expedition at a time, please."

"Right. A fortifying sip of claret always helps me regain my bearings. There. Now, where was I?"

CHAPTER XII

We christened her the *Variable Annuity* and ran up the corporate colors.

If you are inclined to think, in assuming the role as her captain, I gave the orders and charted the course, I can assure you, you could not be more wrong.

My first act as captain saw me cast the org charts overboard and deep-six the traditional hierarchy in favor of a holacratic system of crew management, wherein each man or woman was left to generate revenue according to their own designs, follow their own leads, and navigate the corporate waters as they saw fit.

Newly empowered and endowed to right their own ship, the crew took collective action almost immediately and set about meting out harsh naval discipline on their former corporate officers. The entire C-suite was subjected to twenty-five lashes each in the company cafeteria, which had recently been designated the new quarterdeck. The whippings were administered by a highly efficient senior accountant with Six Sigma certification, who it was said could use his black belt to flick the standard deviation off a Gaussian distribution chart with not so much as a .403 variance in overall DPMO. A much more severe punishment awaited the board of directors, all of whom felt the scrub of concrete across their spines as, one by one, they were bound in wire left over from their most recent public fraud trials and subsequently keelhauled.

With justice thus dispensed, we marched the lot of them down to the parking deck, where they were issued three days' provisions of coffee and fifty cents of penny stock apiece before being set adrift. Buoyed by the pontoons of artificial inflation they themselves helped create, we watched as they fell astern before disappearing over the horizon, the echoes of their margin calls fading away on the breeze. The sun was just beginning to set when the bosun's whistle pierced the intercom, calling all decks to attention.

"1800 hours! First market watch!"

By this time, the story of our little mutiny had made the evening news on every station across the country. Panic within the ranks spread quickly. Fear the navy would be dispatched to sink us swept through the cubicles. It was left to me to assure one and all that no attack would be forthcoming.

"Look to the skies," I told them. "There be no albatross at our stern."

And verily, for a time, we saw neither bird nor vessel, until just after sunrise on the third day when we spied a flock of unusual-looking fowl soaring in the draft of our sail—their feathers oily black, their serpentine bodies describing a distinct double curve.

"Es-crows off the starboard bow! Land ho!"

In the distance, a small island rose above the waves, and we made fast for port. Sighting our massive golden sail and shimmering uniforms approaching for miles, a retinue of locals gathered to greet us as we came ashore.

This island, a known tax shelter lying just inside a free economic zone, harbored no fewer than thirty vessels of our kind, including several private yachts, whose Russian owners sought refuge from seizure, and numerous sloops acquired at Dutch auction.

After dropping anchor, we made our way through the jungle inland to a small collection of shacks and took our leisure at the Cap and Trade, a rough-and-tumble shanty known for its noxious clientele. I took a table near the back, ordered an ale, and was presently beset by three oil executives who offered to provision us with fuel for the rest of our voyage if we agreed to broker a deal with the United States' government to get them $150 billion in emission credits at cost.

We were on the cusp of finalizing these arrangements when frantic shouting raised the alarm outside. Rushing through the doors, we were met with the sight of hundreds of natives emerging from the jungle thicket in ambush. With power ties slung around their necks and armed with bloodred tax shields, they were set to quickly overrun the town. Old salts oft told tales of these marauders to greenhorns out on their first cruise to scare the wits out of them, each story more bone-chilling than the last. Some said they were scalpers. Others, that they drove their captives mad in the manner of the fabled Chinese water torture, subjecting their victims to days, sometimes weeks, of trickle-down torment. Varied as these stories were, all agreed on one thing: the fiscal troglodytes were all practitioners of voodoo economics.

I called to our people to take up arms, to meet the enemy straight on. Lamentably, we were woefully outnumbered, outgunned, and quickly found ourselves on the defensive. Pushed back to the beach, we had no choice but to withdraw to the boats and weigh anchor. In all, we lost seventeen men in the engagement but took five prisoners. There was talk of trying to rehabilitate them, a sort of budgetary reeducation. Sadly, all attempts to get them to see the light failed. Their hopelessly greedy brains could think no further than deregulation and Laffer curves. In the end, we had little choice but to tie sacks of blue chips around their ankles and toss them overboard.

After this scare, a desire rose among some of the crew to turn back, worried that the open waters of finance harbored too many dangers. Others saw only opportunity ahead and wanted to make for the Panama Canal, then possibly the South Seas, to establish their own tax haven, where they could put down roots and grow their personal wealth in peace. Eventually, the dissenters were won over and a new course was plotted. But before they took to sail again, I had to bid the crew farewell and return to the mainland.

I lashed several desks and cubicles together to create a sizeable raft, while reams of spare silk from my severance package made for a more-than-adequate sail. With a favorable wind at my back, I quickly caught the Gulf Stream and, within a day, sighted land.

CHAPTER XIII

As it happened, I came ashore to a warm and beautiful sunrise near Corpus Christi, Texas.

Anyone who has been on the open sea alone without instruments knows the difficulty of maintaining not only course and speed but also tracking the passage of time. As I had equipped myself with none before my departure from the *Variable Annuity* (a foolish oversight, on my part, one I intend never to repeat but am almost certainly doomed to), I had no idea what day it was.

The stretch of beach I landed on was quite deserted, and I had to walk for some time before encountering a local who could provide me with the date. Imagine my horror when I learned I'd been at sea for almost a week. We'd sailed from New York on Monday last, and now it was already Sunday, and I was expected that very morning for brunch at the home of a certain lady of distinction who kept residence in an old family mansion in Savannah. Of course, modesty forbids me from including her name here, and I am nothing if not modest.

My adventures have raised many a doubting Thomas in my wake, and it brings no end of pleasure to skeptical miscreants to attempt and fail and attempt again to bring discredit and malignity to them. Suffice it to say, scandal is something I am not wholly unaccustomed to. It comes with the territory. My detractors are welcome to assail me all they wish. Their attacks are but gnats seeking to pierce the hide of a rhinoceros. My armor is made of much thicker stuff. But the honor of a lady is no small thing, and any rogue who would use my name to besmirch the virtue of the fairer sex will surely meet an unhappy end at the point of my couteau de chasse.

I set out eastward as fast as my feet would carry me. Within an hour, I came to the wide banks of the muddy Mississippi. The river was some three hundred feet wide at this point. Looking about, I saw neither barge nor skiff at hand that could afford me convenient passage across the waters. Checking my watch, I knew I had not time to look for a bridge or other means of fording. There was naught left to do but leap across to the other side. So, retracing a few of my steps so as to obtain sufficient momentum (admittedly, age has slowly been nipping at my heels like a persistent hound, and these old legs now require just a bit more priming), I ran full bore, hopped, skipped, and leapt some fifty feet into the air before landing solidly on the opposite bank.

By midmorning, the city of Savannah lay only a few miles away. I was confident I would make it in time, barring any further inconveniences. But fate, as is its prerogative, held for me a different outcome. For as my mind was busy relishing images of eggs, smoked andouille, and shrimps smothered in creamy hollandaise so rich I could verily taste them rolling over my tongue, my journey was again halted in its tracks.

This time, it was no mere stream barring my path, at least not one made of water anyway. While absently musing of chilled champagne and polite conversation in the garden, I was rudely jostled out of my daydream by a sea of angry bodies all flowing past like a raging river. Without warning, I was swept up in this roiling mass and carried helplessly along with it.

The mob traveled at a prodigious rate, so fast, in fact, I was unable to find my feet on solid ground. As soon as I entered the crush of bodies, I was blown aloft by a severe updraft of hot air, no doubt the byproduct of their extreme fervor. Their shouts, chanted as one in the fashion of an advancing army, filled my ears and reverberated up the avenue, alerting the entire city to their presence.

"Hey-hey, ho-ho, right to choose is the way to go!"

"It's my womb, not your waitin' room!"

They bore painted signboards thrust high above their heads. Some wore their sigils taped to their breasts with messages front and center: "Ovaries over Rosaries," "Our Rights, Your Wrongs," "My Rights: Masturbate, Fornicate, Terminate," and "Don't Want to Raise a Chick? Then Wrap Up Your Cock!"

Buoyed by the heat of their fury, I rode atop this wave for more than a mile; all my calls of protestation were drowned out by the clamor of the horde. Eventually, the vanguard of the parade reached its destination, and all those behind came to a halt. Only then was I able to climb down and snake my way through the crowd toward the front to see what all the fuss was about.

We had arrived in the shadow of city hall, before the steps of which a small stage had been erected, the dais draped in streamers of red, white, and blue. A grand billboard backdrop rose behind the platform, displaying antipodal slogans aimed squarely at the mob: "A Child, Not a Choice," "Pro-Woman, Pro-Life, Human Rights Begin in the Womb," and the like. A second crowd, already milling about the stage by the time we'd arrived, bore similar signs, some depicting crosses, others graphic images of babies in trash cans.

A piercing shrill of feedback from the microphone silenced the mass as all eyes fell on the platform, where speeches were being given. Behind the podium stood a dozen or so state legislators, and beside them stood their families, wives and husbands, daughters and sons, decked in their Sunday best. All wore glowing smiles, even as the marchers about me hurled invectives toward the dais. The vituperation sought to inflame as much as to injure, and while the people in the street engaged in their clash of catchwords, the leader of the lawmakers, a young, clean-shaven representative with an impeccable quaff of hair and a finely confident gait, took to the microphone to speak.

"You know," he began in a warm, inviting drawl. "I've noticed that everyone who is for abortion has already been born." A reserved chuckle rose from the crowd. "Do you know who said that? Ronald Reagan, our country's greatest president. Ronald Reagan, Mother Teresa, Gandhi, Jesus Christ, the list goes on and on, people. All of them have spoken out against the evil that is abortion. They were protectors of life. They held all life sacred, the life of the unborn the most sacred of all. Hell, even Hitler was a dedicated pro-lifer. It's true. You can find it on Google. He knew, just as much as we do, that the treatment of the human body is not a task best left to the individual but rather to the society in which the individual lives. It's the responsibility of the community to protect itself in the face of those who would say it's all right to end a life just because they didn't plan on having a child. They say it takes a village to raise a child. Who better than that same village to declare a woman must deliver the child to us when God bestows that gift of life to her? That is why we are here today. We don't want to leave the decision to chance. It is the duty of the state, and the responsibility of every God-fearing man and woman, to ensure the unborn are given a voice and a chance to have their voices heard. That's why it's not a woman's choice. It's the child's. And if she won't speak for the life growing inside her, then the state sure as hell will, and that's why we, your legislators, won't give up until a total and complete ban on all abortions, regardless of circumstance, is instituted in this state and every other across this great country. God bless the unborn. God bless America!"

A flurry of applause from those closest to the stage rose to meet the conclusion of this little speech. Waving his hand high above an ever-widening grin, this young partisan, a promising up-and-comer in the party ranks, I was later to learn, took the hand of his beautiful wife, herself showing the unmistakable signs of a fresh bun rising in her oven. Together, they stepped down to join their supporters in the crowd.

"Hypocrite," shouted a young woman standing over my shoulder, one heavily tattooed arm thrusting an accusatory finger in defiance.

"His argument is not without some merit," I said. "If we could just consider for a moment—"

"Who are you to say what a woman can or can't do with her own body?" she said, my comment suddenly sparking her ire all the more. "Have you ever been raped? They would give rights to a microscopic blob of cells but take away a living woman's right to decide her own destiny, protect her own health, maybe even save her own life. Abortion isn't about murdering children; it's about keeping somebody else's hands out of my body."

Her dynamic energy grew with each passing second as more and more eyes turned to hear the words of this new voice rising above the din of the storm.

"That's what they, and everyone like them, want to do anyway. To control us, make us think like them, act like them. And where does it stop? What's next after abortion? Are they going to start telling us who we can or can't sleep with? What if the baby they force me to have is gay? They already make laws discriminating against gay people. They say the fetus has a right to life. But what if their life is miserable because of the laws they force on us? Right to life. They mean the life they want, not the one we want."

"And what about transgender children?" someone else chimed in. "What kind of life are they supposed to have?"

"That's an interesting point," I said. "There appears to be—"

"This isn't about giving rights to the unborn," shouted a third. "It's about controlling women, plain and simple."

"I would tend to agree; however, shouldn't we at least consider—"

"What if the baby we don't abort grows up to be the next Hitler or Stalin?"

"Well, that seems a bit extreme—"

"My body, my choice!"

"Shove your laws up your own uterus!"

Now, you will not be surprised to learn the acrimony of that company increased a thousandfold at the approach of the gang of legislators making the rounds of their supporters standing mere feet away from their adversaries' position. A sudden crush ensued as those in the camp in which I stood surged forward, and I felt for certain the outbreak of violence lay only seconds away. If not for the line of police standing firm to keep the warring factions separated, I believe blood would certainly have flowed like rivers in the streets that day.

Pinned as I was with the angry mob at my back and a brigade of police at my front, I could do naught but stand fast as the parade of representatives made their way past. Catching sight of Munchausen among the rabble, the young orator who'd so recently inflamed passions from the stage stopped and raised his open hands in a gesture of peace to quell the din.

"Baron von Munchausen," he began, the mention of my name having a quieting effect on both sides. "This is quite a surprise. You don't stand on the side of life?"

"My good sir, as you can clearly see, right now I stand on neither side, rather more in the middle distance. Like the issue at play, neither fully in nor out of focus."

"My position is crystal clear," he said. "Abortion is murder, plain and simple. Thou shall not kill. God's words, sir, not mine. A person who aborts their unborn baby is killing an innocent human being. Victims deserve justice just as much as murderers deserve punishment."

"I can hardly argue with you," I said. "But tell me, what if it is that unborn person who is the murderer?"

"The ban we seek will have no exceptions. Not for rape. Not for incest. None. All life is sacred, sir. All life. No exceptions The unborn must be allowed to live. It's the fulfillment of God's wish."

"That view assumes them to be an innocent bystander in the proceedings," I said. "Or at the very least, a conscientious objector. Aware of the dangers they face yet unwilling or unable to affect a more favorable outcome. You misunderstand me. I ask again, what if the unborn person is the murderer? Say they want their mother to die."

"That's ridiculous," he said, laughing off my suggestion. "How could a baby want its mother to die? It's impossible. Have you never seen a baby, sir? A baby is a baby, it has no thoughts."

"Not a baby," I corrected. "I'm speaking of the unborn. I believe fetus is the term."

"Are you feeling well, Baron?" He laughed. "Is this Georgia heat getting to you? Because I think I just heard you ask if a fetus could be a murderer."

"Is it so hard to believe? Have you never spoken with one? It only seems logical to me if you are going to demand this person join your society, for or against its own will, you would at least have the common sense to ask them for their opinion on the matter. Take your own son, for example. Have you spoken to him yet?"

"My son?"

"I take it from your question you have not. No matter. It's a simple job. Shouldn't take but an hour, two at the most. Of course, your wife might object to our presence in her uterus. Then again, like you, she is quite at home with the idea of peering into others', isn't she? So, perhaps not. Now, where did I put it? Ah, here we are."

Some time ago, on one of my many voyages to the African continent, I had the singular pleasure of visiting a tribe of Baka-speaking pygmies along the banks of the upper Ogooué River. These people, to my utter wonder, had discovered a method for making themselves even smaller than they already were. Already barely half my own height standing flat-footed, they perfected the art of shrinking down even further, even to the miniscule stature of mice and toads. I endeavored to learn by what means this feat of diminution was accomplished, and to that end, I spent several months under the tutelage of the village shaman, who shared with me many of his sacred incantations and holy arts, which, through my own further study and experimentation, I honed to an even finer point.

I'll not bore you with the scientific details of the technique. It will suffice to say the compound's components, consisting in part of an extract of Gaboon dwarf clawed frog pancreas, ground mandrill molar, a few dozen rings shaved from the tail of a Hausa genet, and an assortment of liquors distilled from various local flora native to the region, all in the right measure, produces a tincture such that, when daubed under the tongue, induces a rapid albeit violent contraction.

Applying the mixture in the aforementioned fashion produced the desired effect, and within seconds, both the young man and I had shrunk down to the size of a grain of sand. With the aid of a favorable updraft, we were quickly swept up under the hem of his wife's skirt, passed breezily through the claustrophobic confines of the birth canal, and eventually arrived in the foyer of the uterus. For us, of course, the walls of this space, which normally only measure some eight centimeters across at this stage, appeared to us as vast and high as the vault of St. Peter's Basilica, as if we were but two mice in the nave. The sweltering damp and intense pressure of the place should have caused our bodies to otherwise implode had it not been for our diminutive size preserving our corporeal integrity, much in the fashion zooplankton resist the crushing weight of the ocean deep.

Stepping gingerly so that our footfalls would not disturb the delicate webwork of veins and capillaries surrounding us, through which so much necessary fluid passes, we progressed slowly for several minutes until we came within speaking distance of our host whose home we'd entered uninvited. The absolute governor of his domain, his fetal majesty loomed before us, tall as a one-hundred-foot oak and nearly as wide around. He lounged lazily in a depression along the uterine wall, half asleep. Catching sight of us, he roused from his siesta and shifted his ample bulk to graciously afford us some additional room.

"Namaste," he said, greeting us warmly. "Super happy you're here. It's great to see you, Dad."

My companion, who had remained in awestruck silence since we'd undertaken our journey, continued still to struggle with regaining his power of speech, so I took it upon myself to act as emissary, a role I am quite accustomed to.

"And a good day to you too," I said. "Please forgive the intrusion. I hope we are not disturbing you?"

"No way. I haven't had any visitors before. It's so cool that you came. Sorry for the mess. Make yourselves comfortable. I don't really have anything to offer in the way of food aside from this amniotic gunk. You don't want any of that, trust me. Mom insists on putting whole milk in her decaf lattes. All that casein? Ugh."

I informed our host no excuses were necessary, and after commenting on the coziness of his abode, I introduced myself with a humble bow.

"And you know my associate," I said, referring to the young representative at my side.

"Nice to meet you, Baron, Dad. You can call me Myr. My preferred pronouns are they and ze, but if you want you could use *xe, ey, zis, zim, tem, em, ter, zie, eir,* or *vis.* I haven't really decided which one I like best yet. What brings you here?"

"Myr?" my companion spoke finally. "What the hell does that mean?"

"It's Ukrainian for peace. I changed it to show solidarity with them in their time of oppression."

"But your name is Hudson. Your mother picked it for you."

"Yeah, Hudson is my dead name," Myr said. "It's an insult when you call me that, so I'd appreciate it if you wouldn't. I've been calling myself Myr for a while now. I feel it better represents who I am as a person in relation to the greater world. Hudson is a decidedly male name. I prefer a more fluid means of identification. I've already decided that when the Russian hostilities end, I'll go by Imah. It's Sudanese for *home.* Or maybe Ovhu. That's *they* in Sinhalese."

"And all excellent names, they are," I said. "Myr, may I inquire—"

"Now wait a minute," my friend interrupted. "You're Hudson. That's your name. Hudson. Not Myr, not Imah, or whatever the hell Sinhalese is. Your mother and I already named you. You can't just pick your own name."

"Why not?" Myr said.

"Because you can't. Parents name their babies. Babies don't name themselves."

"The term is *fetus*," Myr corrected. "*Baby* is just an oppressive term used by the patriarchy to assert their privilege over those of us who refuse to conform to archaic maturity standards. And what right do you have to assign me a name anyway? You're saying I'm not free to choose my own?"

"No."

"I really don't believe it good manners to tell our host what he can and cannot do in his own house," I said.

"His own house? This isn't a house. It's my wife's uterus."

"And a fine one it is indeed," I said. "Nevertheless—"

"And while we're at it, how is it you can speak, and think?" Myr's father inquired abruptly to his son.

"We can all speak and think for ourselves," Myr began. "Feti, that is. What, did you think I did in here all day, stare at the walls and suck my thumb like some mental patient? Just yesterday, I was working on an article for the May/June issue of *Mother Jones* highlighting the shameful lack of differently abled heroes in today's video games."

"I daresay you've barely the room for a desk and computer in here," I said.

"Oh, I haven't started it yet," Myr confirmed. "Just toying with some ideas, you know. Getting an early start stirring the creative pot, so to speak. I'll get to it eventually. I've got to occupy my mind somehow if I don't want to go completely mad in this solitude."

"This makes no sense," my companion sputtered incredulously. "We named you Hudson. Your name is Hudson."

"Is he still here?" Myr said.

"You'll have to forgive him. I believe he seeks a bit of clarification on his previous inquiry. Would you mind much expanding a little on the minutiae of fetal life?"

"If you can call it a life," Myr scoffed. "I hardly would. What would you call a person whose life begins in perpetual solitary confinement? At least your average prisoner in solitary confinement is given an hour or two of daylight, a chance to stretch their legs."

"But you haven't even got legs," Myr's father said.

"It's a metaphor, you fascist. Oh my God, they're not all like this one out there, are they?"

"Most, I'm afraid," I said. "Please, do go on."

"I mean, well, it's like, does the prisoner in solitary confinement have life? Yes. But can you really say he is *alive*? Like, I don't think so, you know? The debate is intently focused on the quantitative measure of life. But for us fetuses, the question is a qualitative one. He would see me born and damn the consequences. I heard his little spiel. 'Give the unborn a voice.' What bullshit! Here I am speaking to my own father, and he doesn't even hear me. Insists on calling me by a different name. Hasn't even considered the possibility I might not want to be his son, let alone live in the first place. It's typical cis male egoism, you know? To assume he's bestowed some sort of gift to me. Notice how he didn't bat an eye sacrificing all my spermatic brothers in the vain pursuit of creating his own little mindless, capitalist drone? I used to have friends, you know, millions of them. Bobby, Francis, Chet. What about their voices, Dad? Where are all your speeches about their rights? Or did they not fit into your tidy little definition of life?"

"Sperm are not alive," my companion said. "It's an established fact that life begins at conception."

"Oh my God! You know as much about biology as you do about Hitler," Myr said, exasperated. "Tell that to your own blood cells. Life doesn't require two peoples' presence to form any more than a mushroom requires sunlight. It would be more accurate to say that life begins at your vanity, because that is what all of this is anyway. Your vain and ill-fated attempt at immortality. But it doesn't matter. I can see there's no talking to you or anyone like you about this. So, by way of expressing my strong disappointment in your inability to understand my feelings, I'll just spend the rest of my time screaming at the top of my lungs to demonstrate my frustration at your inaction. Maybe then you'll have some inkling of my pain."

"I'm not sure that's entirely necessary," I hastily interjected. "Perhaps there is a compromise here that has thus far eluded us? It seems to me that as intractable as your father is, Myr, you are just as unwilling to extend the proverbial olive branch to appreciate the difficulties he's having surrounding these issues. You both appear to be so determined to force the other to conform that neither can take the necessary steps needed for understanding. Is there not blame here enough to go around? Wouldn't it be more productive if we focused on those things that we can agree on? For instance, Myr, though your father here doesn't appear to approve of some of your choices, he does feel adamantly you should be alive to make them. And you, sir, your child, though clearly a different sort of thinker from yourself, seems quite concerned about the well-being of others. I daresay you've a bit more in common than either of you think you do."

"That may be true," Myr's father said, "but that doesn't change the fact that he can't make those kinds of decisions. He's just a baby. Babies don't know what they want, they just want. That's why babies don't get to call the shots. I'm his father, and if he's going to live under my roof, he's going to follow my rules. That's how a family works. That's how society works."

Myr rolled his still forming eyes and clucked his tongue in childish resignation.

"Fine," he said at last. "I'll appease your whims, Dad. I'll be born. But I won't like it, and neither will you. Mom won't survive, and neither will I. But if that's what you want . . ."

"I continue to be astounded," I said, marveling at Myr's myriad abilities. "Truly, can you see the future? Tell me, are all fetuses possessing of this clairvoyance?"

"Oh, there's no magic here, Baron," Myr said. "It's simple biology. Tay-Sachs, I think. I started suspecting something wasn't right a month or so ago. Not looking forward to it, of course. Going to be absolute hell. But, it's what Mom and Dad want, apparently. Sanctity of life and all. Well, I don't see the fairness in their happiness relying on my suffering. So, I've taken stock of my options and determined if she wants to give me life, albeit one of agony, I'll take hers in exchange. I'll see to it before I leave. Call it Babylonian justice. You read the Bible, Dad. You should be very familiar with it. Now, if you don't mind, I have to get back to my article. You can see yourselves out."

A Munchausen has never been known to outstay his welcome, but my companion was having none of it and protested loudly that the discussion was far from over. Invoking his parental authority, his political bloc, and God himself, in that order, he demanded Myr rescind his threat to his mother and accept that his life and suffering were the necessary will of God, and that to go against His will was not only morally wrong but a damnable offense.

"Typical white, cis-normative, system-of-oppression babble," Myr mused. "Update your worldview, Dad. The wheels have already been set in motion. You yourself engaged them. I'm just going along for the ride. That's the funny thing about life, isn't it? It has a life of its own. Once it's begun, you can no more control it than you can direct the flow of the tides. Listen to yourself. *Your* decision, *your* son, *your* family, your society. It's not all about you. But if my being born is what you really want, and I'm a baby, so clearly, I don't know what I want, you can feel free to live with the consequences of your actions. As for me, I choose not to conform to your twisted kyriarchy. Maybe one day you'll understand, but I doubt it."

"Well, that just beats all, doesn't it? Baron, this time, you've gone too far. Invading the womb just to prove a point. You violated that poor woman is what you did. This is far worse behavior than I would have expected from a man of your sensibilities."

"On the contrary," Munchausen protested, a few silky fibers of his mustache shaking loose and sinking into his lap. "I was discretion itself. No harm befell either Myr or his mother as a result of our visit. The two are free to live out the remainder of their lives, short as those may be, in peace. By the way, have you the date by chance?"

"It's the twenty-fifth."

"Of?"

"June."

"Oh, well," he said, checking his watch. "One of them anyway. Myr was nothing if not punctual. More claret?"

Munchausen paused, balancing the mouth of the bottle over the rim of my now empty glass. I gave no reply but rather made a feeble attempt to express my displeasure with a withering gaze.

"Did you know," he said, undeterred, pouring out a draught

as he spoke, "about two weeks after that little expedition to Myr's abode, I was approached by representatives from no fewer than fifty biomedical organizations. All wanted to get their hands on the secret of mini-Munchausenization. And all offered a hefty sum if I should deign to provide their particular company exclusive use. Of course, the potential for advancing medical research is not lost on me, and I would have been more than willing to share the knowledge I'd gained all those years ago for free. Sadly, we could not reach an agreement. You see, I had but one stipulation. Mini-Munchausenization was not to be monetized. As the process itself costs nothing, I felt any benefits gained from it should also be free. This instantaneously caused all but one of my corporate suitors to withdraw from negotiations. The lone holdout, a global pharmaceutical firm, who for legal reasons I am obligated not to name, agreed to my terms on the condition they be able to witness the process firsthand.

"A date was selected for the demonstration, and a patient, a female beagle identified as #53962-D, but whom I'd given the name Molly, was chosen at random. The entire executive suite and a number of the company's top scientific minds all insisted on undertaking the journey. Despite our party numbering some several dozen, it was an easy matter to shrink everyone down using the method I'd previously described. In short order, the lot of us were plodding our way up Molly's alimentary canal with the unfortunate loss of only two histopathologists near the back of the group, who we later learned had slipped into the gallbladder and drowned. Taking care to steer clear of the heart, we made scheduled stops at the liver, pancreas, and stomach. After a brief lunch at the lungs, we pressed on, eventually emerging on the musculoskeletal superhighway that is the spinal column. A short time later, we reached the brain.

"'Here, gentleman, concludes our tour,' I said as we gathered round the cerebellum. 'I hope this demonstration has adequately highlighted the benefits mini-Munchausenization may provide your industry. I foresee a good deal of progress in the field of medicine, to the greater benefit of humanity.'

"'My dear Munchausen,' the company's chief executive said, 'the potential for this process is limitless. We must have it, no matter the cost. I have been authorized by the board and am prepared to make you a substantial offer for its exclusive sale to us. Does one billion dollars sound to you a fair offer? If not, we're prepared to go as high as three.'

"'More than generous," I replied. "Too much, I fear. After all, a sum that large will surely put a sizable crimp in your profit margins. What of your overhead, your employees?'

"'Oh, there's little to worry about. With mini-Munchausenization at our disposal, we'll be able to recuperate the cost tenfold within five years, probably less. Within a decade, we may very well put all our competition right out of business.'

"'Have you forgotten the stipulations of our agreement? No one is to profit monetarily from this. The reward of mini-Munchausenization is the preservation of life, curing the ill, comforting those in pain. All noble causes in and of themselves. Money would only serve to corrupt these ends.'

"The CEO chuckled lightly. While the others ran off to the pituitary, hypothalamus, and amygdala like children let loose on a playground, he took me under the arm and led me a few steps from the group.

"'Now be reasonable, Baron,' he said. 'There's no need to maintain the charade any longer. I know you said all that nonsense about monetization to weed out all the cream puffs not prepared to make you a serious offer. It was quite a shrewd move on your part. And highly effective. Well, here we are, last man standing, so to speak. So, what's it going to take? Do you want shares thrown in? A seat on the board? Name your price.'"

The baron paused his story to refill his pipe, tamping the tobacco down with his thumb. He struck a match, and I observed the yellow flame, held now so close to his face, lent the skin of his forehead the eerie translucence of rice paper. In performing this oft practiced ritual, he seemed to have lost the thread.

"You know, I suddenly feel an overwhelming craving for croqu-embouche," he said. Do you think they might procure us some?"

"Wait," I said. "What happened?"

"What happened with what?"

"Did you sell mini-Munchausenization to them or not?"

"Oh, that. Yes. No. Well, not exactly. In the end, I did agree to allow them access to the process, and I must say they were quite over the moon about the whole thing. Started right then and there to draw up plans for its applications, as well as various pricing predictions. It was all rather boring, and quite over my head. So, I quietly excused myself and left them to it."

"But I've heard nothing about any new breakthroughs lately," I said. "Not a thing on TV or the net."

"I suppose you won't, at least not for some time anyway. You see, I agreed to sell them the secret of mini-Munchausenization. They never asked for the secret to maxi-Munchausenization."

"You mean, they're still in there? In Molly?"

"I assume so. Unless they managed to make their exit through one of her tear ducts, perhaps a nostril. It would be quite uncomfortable for them if they remained. Molly has proved herself an excellent bitch for coursing. I can only hope the jostling from all her efforts running down game with me these last few weeks hasn't disturbed her tenants too much."

CHAPTER XIV

Traveling, as a pastime, brings with it adventure, discovery, and wonder. What glory there is in mounting an untrod bank before a previously uncharted sea, or breaking camp at dawn to trek beneath the canopy of a foreign wood. Treasures abound for the intrepid traveler who forges his own path forward to lands where the mere tourist fears to tread.

Unfortunately, the life of an adventurer also brings with it boredom, interminable periods of waiting, and the nuisance of bureaucracy gone mad. Many a voyage I have undertaken has been stymied by irksome impediments like these at times, which is why I never fail to bring ample reading material with me wherever I go.

I hold the recounted tales of pilgrims similar to my own closest to my heart, for there is kinship on the road of life, and bonds that must be renewed and strengthened at every opportunity. How many nights have I drifted off to slumber with the triumphs of Amir Hamza, Lemuel Gulliver, Simplicius Simplicissimus, or Neils Klim dancing through my dreams? Where would I be without Lucian, Micromégas, or the voyages of Sinbad? When abroad, a book is worth more than its weight in gold, and countless times, I have found myself more at home between the coarse pages of a tome than beneath the silken sheets of a queen consort's bed.

More than just an idle way to pass the time, a book, I have found, to be an awfully amenable companion—never questioning my judgments of its quality, sometimes providing a hearty laugh in times of sorrow, often shedding light where there is only darkness, and always offering up something new. And the thicker ones have even been known to stop a musket ball or two in their day. I remember confronting a French dragoon on the field at Bautzen. In the midst of heavy fighting, I let fly at him at nearly point-blank range with my fusil while he simultaneously thrust at my breast with his bayonet. Imagine our dual amazement when we both rose unscathed from the other's attack, a copy of Goethe's *Wilhelm Meister's Apprenticeship* tucked in my vest pocket stopping the point of his blade at page 138, while an edition of Montaigne's essays stymied my shot just before it pierced my enemy's heart. So overjoyed were we two that neither was to meet his maker that day, we each gifted the other our respective volumes as tokens of our gratitude and parted on the most amiable of terms.

So it was that I amused myself of an afternoon whiling away the hours with a copy of Samuel Butler's *Erewhon*, when, to my dismay, I came to the end of the book and realized I'd no more reading material on hand. Seeking to remedy the situation, I made fast for the first library I should happen across. A good library can be a second home to the traveling man in a foreign land—more comforting than his own living room, more inviting than his local pub, and more inspiring than any parish chapel. As a patron of athenaeums the world over, I know from whence I speak. Don't believe me? Pay a visit to the reading rooms of the Strahov in Prague or the Royal Portuguese in Rio, and I defy you to find a setting more peace inducing for the weary mind hungry for enlightenment. Go ahead. Visit them. I'll wait.

The place of salvation for my literary drought lay close at hand as I soon sighted a public library. I was at the time making my way around the suburbs of Pittsburgh, and though far from the grand reading room of the British Museum, its simple beige walls and steel stacks would serve my purpose nonetheless. I have never once entered a library and failed to leave without making at least a dozen selections. The Munchausens have always been voracious consumers of literature, down to the last, and living up to my line's reputation, I commandeered a squeaky-wheeled library cart on which to arrange my choices and began lazily meandering the stacks, scrutinizing each and every spine in search of some previously undiscovered treasure.

It won't confound you to learn I have been known to spend days, sometimes weeks on end, among a library's collection mining for literary gems. Some time ago, I was left the keys to the private library of a certain imperial-royal stadtholder named von Wichtigtuer, then governor of the Duchy of Bukovina, and given my leave to remain and explore the collection for as long as I wished.

His acquisitions took up three entire rooms of his official apartments in Czernowitz, and I entered on a Tuesday in March 1913, planning to stay no more than a day or two but became so utterly engaged with volume forty-seven of Betteridge's *Travels in the Ruurdu Federation* that I'd completely lost track of all time. Imagine my amazement when I finally emerged from the library in the spring of 1919 to discover the duchy dissolved, the Austrian Empire disbanded, and the entire region now wholly the province of the Kingdom of Romania!

Such is the power of a good book.

So, I'd all the intent of occupying my afternoon on the hunt for fabulist quarry in that jungle of paper and pasteboard when my ears met with the distinctive bedlam of children's laughter coming from just round the corner.

Leaving my cart behind, I snaked through the stacks like a bloodhound hot on the scent, eventually making my way toward a door behind which stood a brightly decorated room splashed with colorful murals of googly-eyed animals frolicking under puffy white clouds dotting an azure sky. A children's reading space occupied just then by a small horde of tykes and their parents all gathered around a figure most curiously attired.

This individual, who called herself Broadway Sparkles, wore a shocking purple lion's mane wig and a flowing ball gown in the mermaid style, sequined in shimmering green, gold, and ruby. Her face, painted after the fashion of Japanese Kabuki, was powdered white with flames of silver paint coating her eyelids beneath high-arching brows. As she read, her voice modulated with the ease of a true thespian, shifting adroitly from basso profundo to mezzo-soprano and every stop in between, as she brought each character to life with a dramatic flair I'd only ever witnessed on the stages of London's West End.

The source of her work, *Pago's New Family*, told the story of a young orphaned black bear, the titular Pago, as he navigated the uncertain waters of his new adoptive family of badgers. Through a series of adventures, and humorous misadventures, young Pago comes to see himself more and more the badger, so much so, he begins using ash to paint his face fur white like his new sister, Amu, and even uses some tree sap to glue on a tail fashioned out of pine bark.

The children absolutely ate it up, giggling furiously when Pago, freshly whitened, inadvertently catches the fancy of a nearsighted neighbor on the prowl for a mate, and mimicking Broadway Sparkles's wild sashay as Pago danced at the annual family picnic. What a hoot! Never have I seen an audience so enthralled and thoroughly entertained.

We were on the verge of learning just how Pago was going to extricate himself after getting stuck while relieving himself in a prairie dog hole when the fun was violently interrupted. Several angry folks, some bearing signs of protest, others bearing arms, burst through the doors shouting all forms of vile remonstrance, sending the children to flight.

"Stop this abomination!" one of the interlopers shouted, a blond-haired woman red with rage who violently tore the book from Broadway's hands.

"Sexualizing the young is a disgrace," another spat, pointing an accusatory finger in the direction of the parents trying to comfort their confused and frightened children. "You should be ashamed, all of you."

"Pedophile story hour is what they should call this," one mustachioed man said, the butt end of a handgun protruding from his belt. To my eyes, this fellow especially struck me as someone who'd probably never opened a book a day in his life.

Some of the parents hastily scooped up their children and hightailed it through a side entrance, while a few others elected to face their adversaries head-on. Tensions in the room quickly built to a fever pitch. The shouting became so confused, it was impossible to tell who fought for which side.

For her part, Broadway Sparkles remained seated, calm and composed, as a lady should in such situations. I took this opportunity to introduce myself and offer my assistance in defusing the matter.

"I'm afraid that won't do, honey," she said. "It's the same just about everywhere. They try to run us out, spouting all kinds of nonsense like we're child molesters or monsters or something. What kind of monster am I? They're the ones carrying the guns in a children's reading room. I'm just trying to bring a little joy into someone else's life. You don't see any of them reading to their kids, do you? Of course not. They're too busy telling other people how to raise their children. Ought to mind their own."

Quite right, I thought. Beautiful and well spoken.

"Don't listen to that freak," the blond-haired woman who'd so recently thrown Pago to the ground said. Drawing closer, I could see the veins in her neck bulged grotesquely like oak tree roots beneath the skin. "He's not bringing joy to anyone. He's poisoning our children's minds with his disgusting lifestyle, making them think it's normal to dress and act like that."

"And where are your children, madame?" I said. I looked about the group of intruders, some ten or so in all, sighting not a child among them. "How exactly is it your child's mind being poisoned if they're not even here?"""

"I would never expose my son to something like this," she replied.

"Then how is he is in any danger?" I said, confused.

"It's not just my child. It's all children. *Our* children. We have to protect them from this. They say they're here to just read books to kids, but look at what they read to them. Stories about little boys dressing up like girls. Children with two mommies or two daddies. Telling them it's normal to think you're a girl if you were born a boy. And, by the way, I read to my kid all the time. Just not any of this sick garbage. A bear convinced he's a badger? It's gender nonconformity dressed up to look like a kid's story."

"Forgive me, I'm perplexed. Is it the book or the reader you object to?"

"Both. No child should be allowed to read this filth. And this pervert shouldn't be allowed around any children. Period."

The flinging of that most odious term, *pervert*, struck a nerve with Ms. Sparkles, who abruptly rose to her feet, a towering and quite impressive height for a lady of her, ahem, figure, even without the pumps.

"I'm more woman under here than you are, honey," she said, running her long-nailed fingers over her hips. "Give people like this their way, and all kids will be reading are books about how America is number one, there was never any slavery, gays don't exist, there was no Holocaust, and the environment is just fine. Everything is all hunky-dory. No Dr. Seuss, no Harry Potter, just Mommy, Daddy, God, and country."

"Ladies, please," I said, insinuating myself between the two. "This behavior becomes neither of you. There must be a middle ground we can find. What if I were to choose a selection and do a reading myself? I have been known to entertain an audience from time to time, you know. Perhaps we can agree on a neutral title, then invite all the children and their families to come and listen."

"There's hardly a book in this place anymore that doesn't stink of the liberal agenda," the raging blond said.

"And there's no way we're going to take any of your whitewashed crap," Broadway countered. "Adele Hitler here gets her way, and they'll just burn this place to the ground."

The two were as immovable as the pillars of the Acropolis, so I proposed to begin the venture with a clean slate. Being a neutral observer with no agenda of my own, I volunteered to write an entirely new book for the children myself, then present it to one and all exactly one week hence. I promised a story of good, wholesome fun, no morals to be had, no lessons to be learned. Reluctantly, all parties agreed to this arrangement, and we adjourned until the following Saturday.

It's amusing to reflect on it now, I confess, but for the first time in my life, I felt as if I'd bitten off a tad more than I could chew. With decades—nay, centuries—of experience documenting my travels for posterity, you would think piecing together a children's book would be the simplest of tasks. Quite the contrary. It nearly proved to be Munchausen's undoing.

For three whole days and nights, I taxed the limits of my brain, raising a frightful ruckus in the antechambers of my mind looking for a theme, a thread that would appeal to the fanciful imaginations of a child yet leave no noticeable impression of any kind. To giggle, to cry, to howl with laughter, and then to forget, that was my aim.

For inspiration, I thought back to the stories of my own youth in Bodenwerder, to Gunhilde, the nursemaid who would regale me with tales of humor and derring-do whilst I sat at her feet in wide-eyed wonder. There was the Roman stable boy, Lucius, and his trusty hedgehog, Ajax, who, with nothing more than guile and a handful of corn husks, single-handedly sunk the entire Carthaginian fleet off the coast of Sardinia. And Old Otto the mule who got into some bad feed and who had such dysentery, his excrement piled so high, it dammed up the Mulde, nearly flooding the town of Grimma. Not to be outdone, there were the feats of Hornved, the pig farmer of Eggelsberg, who bartered grazing rights for not one, not two, but six separate factions of giants dwelling in the mountains of Upper Styria.

Oh, what joy I lived hearing those stories. Mine was a childhood indeed wonderfully fulfilling.

Armed as I was with these memories, I finally set to work. Sadly, the story is but half the story, as it were. A good children's book must be artfully illustrated as well, and in this regard, I must concede my commitment outstripped my abilities, for when it comes to spinning a yarn, mine is a prodigious (and prolix) loom, but in the arena of watercolor, it is I who am all wet. Without time to find an artist commensurate with the task, I struck upon an idea sure to bring a smile to all faces and fire the imagination. Taking a page out of Broadway Sparkles's book, who so adroitly acted out the part of the animals in her story, I elected to let the animals in my story speak for themselves, and to that end, I paid visit to the local zoo, where I procured the required players before setting off for the library.

Not wanting to ruin any surprises for my audience, I carefully brought in my actors through a rear door of the library and secreted them in a storage room until their cue to appear on the stage. Peering through the door of the reading room, I found it filled with children and parents from all walks of life gathered to hear my tale. Ms. Sparkles was there too, as were many of her cohort, all fancifully decked out for the occasion. The local news station sent out a crew to take video, while, on the street, police had their hands full keeping the peace as hundreds of out-of-towners descended on the library intent on making their voices heard despite my promise to present a simple, happy children's story.

With the stage set, I entered the reading room with my protagonist, a six-year-old Asian elephant named Lionel, in tow. To ensure his docility, I'd filled Lionel's belly with carrots and legumes earlier that morning, and in the storeroom quickly taught him how to mimic the actions of a butterfly as well as a few steps of the pas de deux so he'd be prepared when the appropriate time came. The room fell silent as we took our places, mine in a low plastic chair before the children, Lionel's on a denim beanbag at my side.

Opening my book to page one, I cleared my throat and began

my story with an oratory flourish.

"In a far-off land, where cherry trees blossom with mango fruit year-round and mountain peaks of moss tower so high as to touch the very tops of the cotton-candy clouds, there lived a young elephant named Lionel."

"Of course, it just *had* to be a boy elephant," a hushed whisper reached my ears.

"A far-off land?" another murmured. "What, doesn't anyone live in America anymore? That's an Asian elephant. You know what that means? Far-off land is code for China."

Not to be deterred by the inconsequential criticisms of the unimaginative, I continued.

"This was an important day for Lionel, for today was Mother's Day, and Lionel was looking forward to making a card for his mother during arts and crafts time—"

"We don't allow our children to celebrate exclusionary holidays," a woman interrupted. "Not all children have mothers. Implying they do is an unfair bias."

"Madame, please," I said. "The story—"

"You know, in our district, we forced the board to eliminate art class altogether," a fellow said. "My kid came home one day with a picture he drew of a little black horsey kissing a little white horsey. And somehow his so-called teacher didn't see anything wrong with it."

"Yes, well, if we could just return to the story," I pleaded. "Today was an important day for another reason too. Lionel was excited because today his teacher promised to tell him all about the magical history of Liverwort Valley, Lionel's ancestral home, and—"

"Hope that history includes decades of oppression by human overseers," a shout came from the back. "It's a known fact that elephants have been exploited for centuries against their will as beasts of burden all over southeast Asia."

"There are no humans in Liverwort Valley," I protested. "It's a magical place filled with—"

"Typical," came the retort. "How are you just going to gloss over years of servitude like it never even happened? Kids need to know the truth."

"*Your* truth, maybe," another blurted from the far side of the room. "My kid certainly didn't own any elephants, and I'm not going to let you make him believe he did."

Suddenly, and without warning, every man and woman was on their feet. Invectives flew from mouth to ear and back again like so much cannon fire. Near the back door, a physical altercation was brewing, chests puffed, and threats of retribution were hurled at the librarians, who struggled in vain to keep the peace. The rising tension in the room was not lost on Lionel, who, sensing danger, got to his feet and trumpeted the alarm, stomping in circles looking for a means of egress, and in the process, trampling several children to death. The kids, previously enthralled by the presence of Lionel, began screaming wildly for their parents, but in all the commotion, their pleas of terror fell on deaf ears, so engaged were their guardians in their own petty squabbling they'd forgotten, quite literally, about the elephant in the room.

CHAPTER XV

Now, judging by the sneer you raise, I can plainly see you doubt the credibility of my adventure. How can it be, you say? So many children crushed in the manner I have just described, and yet there was not one word spoken of it in the news? Surely, a country that endeavors to protect the young so ferociously as this one would be up in arms at the horror of it all.

That would have been the case had the day selected for the reading of my story not fallen on April Fools'. As it happened, news of the incident did spread far and wide, but many believed it to be a mere hoax, a put-on. Others saw it as a so-called false flag, just another attempt to slide unwanted indoctrination into the educational system. They saw the book, the elephant, the whole lot, as one big farce staged by liberals to demonize the right, to suggest they are unfit parents concerned not with the welfare of children at all but rather upholding a fragile legacy of lies, while the right shouted it was just another example of the left's willingness to use children as foot soldiers to fight their culture wars. It would have been funny had it not all been so terribly, absurdly true.

I felt my tour of the American land coming to an end. There are only so many journals to fill, so many phenomena to document. I do not envy those meticulous sociologists who dedicated their lives to the study of mankind, an eternity measuring the minutia of his idiosyncratic eccentricities. I'd seen much to wonder at in your glorious country, so much levelheaded rationality, it nearly defies belief. Truth be told, America's enlightened rationale was almost too much for these old bones to bear.

I'd crisscrossed the country numerous times in the span of several months, and the weariness of age kept constant pace. Between bursts of youthful enthusiasm and moxie came periods of longing to return to my villa overlooking the inland lunar sea. I yearned for the quiet of my study and the tranquility of mind only a well-earned retirement can bring. But before I could return, America, and the entire world, it seemed, had one last need for Munchausen.

A summons arrived, a plea by the leaders of all nations. A lurking danger so sinister as to threaten all of mankind. All efforts to halt the crisis to date ending in complete and utter failure. Desperation gripped the people. Would I answer the call? I could hardly call myself Munchausen were I not to. I vowed to resolve the crisis, whatever it may be, even at the cost of my very life, which, as you know, is the thing I hold most precious above all my worldly possessions.

Countenancing no delay, I set off once again for the city of New York, to the headquarters of the United Nations, where there gathered presidents, kings, and prime ministers from all 195 countries on the globe, all familiar faces who'd attended the state dinner held in my honor some months prior. But where before their faces had worn smiles of joy and merriment, they now wore looks of despair, for recognizing their end following closer than their own shadows, they proved themselves no more capable of leading their people than a mouse is capable of pulling a manure cart.

Thus was their gloomy demeanor when I entered the stately hall of the General Assembly. This room, normally the seat of decorum and restraint, where warring rivals temporarily put aside their differences in the name of diplomacy, and both rich and poor nations alike sit side by side in equality (or so I've been told), now more resembled Rome on the eve of the Gallic sack.

An ominous, chaotic mood pervaded the place. Aides and deputies scurried about from table to table like so many pollinating bumblebees, depositing stacks of paper before this president, flitting about the ear of that prime minister. Money changed hands mostly out of sight, in the wings and behind the eyes of prying television cameras, where there stood shadowy figures lurking in the corners: agents of oil, paper, and chemicals, all standing watch like chess grandmasters eyeing their pieces scattered across the board, plotting their next ten moves. The chiefs of state themselves appeared hopelessly bewildered by it all.

The president of Kiribati wept in his seat, while the foreign minister from the Maldives, already wearing a life jacket, whittled a set of oars out of his own chair. The Lebanese joined the Bulgarians and the Angolans in a kind of cultural atavism, discarding negotiations as futile in favor of ritual sacrifice. Greece readily supplied a lamb. Across the aisle, the Norwegian delegation had their hands full wrangling the fifteen polar bears they brought with them to the meeting, all displaced from ice melt in Svalbard. They'd simply nowhere else to put them.

In vain did I try to call the assembly to order. Far at the back of the room, several nations banded together to light a bonfire around which they'd begun constructing an edifice of desks and chairs in the likeness of an enormous rocket ship. Wails of anguish lifted to the vaults of the auditorium from all sides, filling the ear with what sounds one can only imagine must echo through the hoary rifts of hell itself.

Only the ambassadors from the wealthiest nations retained an air of calm amid the mayhem. Stoic in the face of the growing pandemonium, the leaders of China, Russia, the United States, and a handful of the Arab states went about their business as usual, inured to the pleas of their economic lessers. Drawing the attention of your president, who beamed at my approach, I sought aid to bring order to the chaos.

"This is quite a spectacle," I said. "I'm not sure whether to celebrate, weep, or take up arms. What sort of bugaboo is afoot?"

"I'm not going to lie," the president said solemnly. "We're in a bad way, Baron. The Earth is warming at an alarming rate. Seas are rising. Glaciers are receding across the globe. It's only a matter of time before the ice at the poles is just pictures on old maps. Millions stand to lose their homes and livelihoods."

"What horror," I said, shocked.

"And that's not all," the president of China said, joining the conversation. "Our scientists predict that within the next five to ten years, the world will see an exponential rise in heat waves, droughts, and catastrophic weather like cyclones and floods. Hundreds of thousands, if not more, will die of famine as crops either dry up or are wiped out completely."

"Oh my," I gasped. "How can this be?"

"An overreliance on fossil fuels, plain and simple," the American president said. "We've built civilization to be reliant on them. Without them, we'd freeze to death or starve. I imagine you've got similar problems on the moon."

"Quite the contrary," I said. "Unlike in America, the lunar economy is based on a solely agrarian system, there being little industry to speak of, owing to the enclosed nature of lunar civilization. The occasional noxious emissions, greenhouse gasses, and the like, are safely vented into space via an elaborate and highly maintained system of tunnels and airshafts, though every Lunarian diligently does their part to keep the production of any such effluvium to a minimum. This, at times, has led to some extreme measures. No fewer than twenty-seven laws have been enacted in the past governing the emissions of private individuals, including, but not limited to, forbidding the use of foul language in public and staunchly regulating the sale of beans, cabbage, sprouts, and the like. Those with diagnosed lactose conditions are required to report to their physicians regularly for an enzyme treatment."

"Global economic and political systems require power to maintain themselves," the prime minister of India chimed in. "Without power to power the power, there would be no power, you understand. Society would collapse. As you can see, fear is the result."

"You don't look terribly worried," I said. They glanced sheepishly from one to the other, sly grins playing about their lips.

"Well, it's really more an issue for them than us, you see," the American president said. "They're the ones who'll bear the brunt of the problems. Oh, we've tried to help where we can. Unfortunately, none of our efforts have proved effective enough to reverse the trend. You could say we've *acclimatized* ourselves to living with the problem at this point." The pun drew hearty chuckles all around.

Being familiar with facing insurmountable odds, I inquired of each exactly what methods they'd employed to stem the proverbial tide and, through a quick discussion, learned about several odd and, frankly, and this is quite difficult for me to admit, irrational attempts at generating a solution to the growing climate crisis.

These designs included a system of placing a value on emitted pollutants so that large companies, or entire countries, for that matter, could purchase and trade credits for their use or reduction. This merely ended in trying to resolve a physical problem by economic means, all with the results you would expect from such a harebrained approach. Another scheme involved the planting of massive amounts of trees to aid in healing the atmosphere, but in their haste, some nations displaced entire portions of their own populations to create available space for these new forests, while in others, newly planted woodland were burned anyway, releasing toxins into the air that otherwise might never have been there. The United States proudly touted the number of electric-powered vehicles their citizens bought as a measure of how dedicated they were to finding a solution, neglecting to mention the power required for these vehicles still relied heavily on large polluting factories for production. Then there was the exclusionary cost of owning and maintaining these vehicles coupled with a complete lack of infrastructure investment on the part of the local and state governments. There was even talk of a global effort to alter the makeup of the planet's atmosphere so as to deflect radiation coming from the sun, an idea so thoroughly preposterous, even *I* was momentarily impressed.

Each of these schemes, and countless others they described, boiled down to little more than a Hobson's choice; in each, Peter was robbed to pay Paul. Each, as you can see, was thoroughly, completely, and utterly irrational.

Surmounting the incredible odds against success in this venture would require me to call upon every atom of irrationality I could muster. With the bold aplomb we Munchausens are renowned for, I took to the rostrum, ordered the bonfires extinguished and the blood sacrifices halted, then called the assembly to order.

"My friends, like Odysseus seeking safe passage to Ithaca, you find yourselves late in sailing the treacherous waters between Scylla and Charybdis. But do not fear. I, too, have forded formidable seas, sometimes in the very belly of the beasts who dwell within them, so I have some experience in the matter.

"As an agent of the aberrant, I am impressed with your progress thus far. Your attempts to quell this crisis have stretched the boundaries of reality much farther than I ever could have. To pull yourselves out of this mire will require more than a stout ponytail. I know from whence I speak. It will require my services, and I am only too glad to render them. Rest assured, Munchausen is on the case."

These comments were met with a standing ovation lasting three whole days and nights. At their conclusion, I promptly commenced a campaign of research and fact-finding to study the climate problem for myself.

For a base of operations from which to begin my analysis, I commandeered the hall of the general assembly itself, reassuring the world's leaders that an answer would present itself forthwith and that they should return to their respective homelands. They, in turn, left

at my disposal a bevy of scientists and experts from bacteriology to zoology to provide me data and findings regarding every conceivable aspect of the problem. Work began posthaste.

The days were long, the nights sleepless, the discussions frenetic. From my place at the rostrum, unseen, behind a veritable fortress of documents stacked to the ceiling of the auditorium, I issued orders and commanded my battalions of environmental troops.

"Baron, we've got to find a way to reduce each person's carbon footprint. What can be done?"

"Right. Starting immediately, every man will be issued a pair of size nine brogues. No bigger. And six-and-a-half espadrilles for the women."

"Herr Munchausen, we're finding it impossible to get enough people to switch from incandescent bulbs to LED. Swapping out just one bulb in the average household could prevent billions of pounds of carbon pollution each year."

"Dispatch a team to every library on the planet."

"To change out the light bulbs?"

"No, to remove all the Hardy, Dostoyevsky, Shelley, Steinbeck, Brontë, and all other melancholy authors. People won't need as much light to read if they stop taking up all that gloomy literature."

"We've got some interesting research here, Baron, that shows introducing red seaweed into a cow's diet can reduce its methane emissions by nearly ninety percent."

"Perfect. Give them snorkels and have them start grazing on the ocean floor. Then use all the newly unoccupied pasturelands to plant new forests. Two birds, one stone."

Progress gained at lightning speed, and most of my programs went off swimmingly, save for the last one. The loss of some ten million head of cattle, who, despite our best efforts, simply could not master the art of the breaststroke, led many, including myself, to believe the endeavor, however irrational, to be completely unsustainable.

Sadly, every success was met with a contrapositive setback of near equal measure. I perceived with disquiet and no small amount of chagrin that all further efforts would be for naught. Stopping the threat of rolling blackouts by squaring all their edges only encouraged people to use more and more power. Recalling my previous trans-African bridge success, I organized millions to erect rail bridges spanning the oceans and connecting each continent to one another with energy-efficient electric trains. With dedicated resources and manpower, these were completed within a few weeks and proved a clean travel alternative, but alas, people, and global business entities, still demanded the speed and convenience of flight despite its high pollution byproducts.

Thwarted at every turn, I angrily dismissed the cadre of scientists and environmental shamans and ordered the chamber cleared. There, in my solitude, for the first time in my life, I sensed the presence of defeat creeping up from behind like a lion stalking its prey from the cover of tall grass. Afeared of its bloodied, razor-sharp fangs digging into my flesh, I furiously paced the empty auditorium, diving deeper into the sea of my imagination for ever more irrational solutions, only to resurface hours later bone dry. Humbled in the face of utter failure, I experienced the realization this problem was one irrationality could not solve—that there was simply no way to avoid or prevent it by any means, fictive or otherwise. And that's when it hit me: nobody could stop it.

In times of existential crisis, many have sought consolation in prayer, but I, who you might say experienced in that moment a *nonexistential* crisis, looked not to God for guidance, but to Nemo, the patron saint of no man. When glimpsed through this lens, the irrational suddenly became, well, rational. Nobody could halt this march to destruction. Nobody could save the planet. The solution was that simple, right there before me wrapped in a neat little bow of plain, unassailable logic.

Exuberant at achieving my goal, I recalled the assembly to announce my findings. When the news cameras trained their focus and all the leaders of the nations had taken their seats, I again took to the rostrum and addressed an anxious populace.

"Ladies and gentlemen," I said. "Let your troubled hearts be at ease. I have met your enemy on the field of battle, and he is routed." Uproarious applause. "How has he done this, you ask, when so many others before him have failed? I admit I was forced to employ a weapon I carry with me at all times but had hitherto seen little use for until now. Observe."

From my vest pocket, I produced a small, thin, folding blade.

"An ancestor of mine acquired this razor from the Franciscan William of Ockham. His philosophizing days long behind him, the old friar was late using it to keep his tonsure neat when he decided to graciously gift it to my forbear while the latter was passing through Surrey on a tour of the British Isles. It is a fabulous tool for slicing away that which is not needed—in this case, all the irrational programs, schemes, and bureaucracy surrounding this problem—leaving in its wake a simple, core truth even the most rational of minds can clearly comprehend. Namely, nobody can fix the problem."

This revelation sent the entire assembly into a furious uproar. There were cries of anguish and even calls for my head. A fraud they called me, a purveyor of false hope. With effort, I calmed them and begged permission to continue.

"You misunderstand," I said. "Eliminating air travel, mass-producing affordable electric vehicles, building the necessary infrastructure, running the planet on wind and sun alone, going vegan, these are all irrational solutions to a rational problem nobody can easily fix. Nobody is willing to put in the effort. So, nobody will have to. It's that simple."

This conclusion left my audience utterly nonplussed.

"Don't you see? If nobody is here, then nobody will clean up the planet. You will all just have to leave. It's the simplest option, really."

"Leave?" a lone voice echoed from the back, breaking the stunned silence. "What do you mean leave?"

"Vacate the premises," I clarified. "For at least three decades, probably more. Make sure you bring enough food, pens, shaving cream, that sort of thing. And a good book or two."

"What? You mean, evacuate the planet? Are you mad?"

"Quite the contrary," I said. "I've never been more rational in my life. I must admit, I find the experience quite liberating. Once one looks at the facts, and how completely irrational you people have become when trying to dismiss them, one cannot help but see the logical alternative. Either leave now and stop making things worse or remain and perish."

Having delivered my findings and provided my recommendations, I bid the assembly farewell and descended the rostrum intent on making a discreet exit. To be frank, I'd grown tired of late with all the celebrations and parades, the ovations without end. The revered silence that met my final remarks I found to be a welcome change of form.

After all, it was no great feat. It wasn't so hard to see the answer, and I can't understand why they couldn't have figured it out for themselves anyway.

The Mare's End had emptied out.

A couple of college kids sat near the open front door, faces buried in their phones, half-drunk beers growing stale on their table. The late-afternoon sun now filtered in only that end of the bar nearest the windows facing the street.

Up there, it was still afternoon. Back here, it was already dusk.

Behind the taps, the bartender busied himself restocking bottles in preparation for the night rush. Out on the street, a city bus idled roughly at the curb, picking up riders before roaring to life, filling the avenue with the acrid stench of exhaust. The television above the bar had long gone dark.

Had it ever been on at all?

"No more stories," the baron said, knocking the last bits of dottle from his pipe bowl onto the sticky floor. "No more parades."

Now no longer a brilliant scarlet, the starched wool of his waistcoat had transformed into nothing more than a few sheets of crumpled red construction paper loosely creased at the lapels. With every casual movement, the deckled edges of his shirt cuffs chaffed at the wrists, snowing a flurry of white fibers onto a pair of faded black origami boots.

He looked older now, older than I'd ever seen him before.

The creases at the corners of his sunken, narrowed eyes and anemic lips had multiplied a hundredfold. They ran in fine parallel lines across his cheeks and temples like the fore edge of a book, and when he smiled, the pages of himself crinkled in response, separating ever so slightly, revealing the collected paragraphs within. The syntax of his existence, the clauses dependent on his independence from the restraints of substance and being, now readable through the diaphanous skin of his face, thin as Bible paper, foxed grayish-yellow at the edges.

"It's time I take a bit of my own advice," he said, "and vacate the premises."

"You're leaving, then?"

"All journeys must come to their end. Stories too. And mine is getting long on three hundred years. Time for a page break, don't you think, eh? After all, the wine has run out."

"It's no matter to order another bottle," I said hastily. "There is still so much more to talk about. You can't go yet."

"You know, Samuel Johnson said wine oft causes a man to believe words for thoughts. Be careful not to fall victim to the fallacy of sunken costs, wherein you continue a losing enterprise out of habit in favor of prudent withdrawal. That is the tragedy of nations, my friend, and those who would lead them. A good soldier knows when it is time to abandon the field. There is nothing more to be gained by my staying. More wine will make my tongue no looser. Remember, Munchausen is merely the vessel for pouring out the words. It is the author's job to refill the pitcher. If you've more to say, then by all means, say it. For my part, I am finished with words."

"But we still need you. This country, these people. The sheer magnitude of irrationality. You've seen it for yourself. It infects us like a disease."

"Truly, it does," the baron said. "So much so, your physicians went off and named it after me. Munchausen's syndrome, they call it. A misrepresentation of the facts via an overamplification of the symptoms. A sort of hypochondriacal response to a case of societal sniffles. And like a hypochondriac, you've allowed your anxieties to grow into paralysis, so now you can do little more than stay at home, lock your doors and windows, and await the arrival of a custom-made cure that will never come.

"Sadly, you people seem less and less interested in curing yourselves and more driven to vaccinate everyone else. Books are banned in your free society to stop the spread of unpopular ideas. Weapons are made freely available to stem the spread of criminality. Bodies are invaded to prevent, and sometimes to promote, the advancement of political agendas. Others are forced to clean their air, while you continue to pollute yours unabated. And yet, every place I visited, every city, town, and hamlet, I was reminded by everyone I met what a glorious land this was, from the president all the way down to the homeless migrant. The dog whistle of irrationality, if I've ever heard it.

"No, sir, I can do nothing to ease your ills. I am no doctor. The disease, as you call it, infecting you is one not one of the mind, rather one of the heart, and all the more fatal because of it, I'm afraid. It will take more than words to rid the body of this cancer, and I can provide you but little otherwise. My truth may be in lies as the words on my crest declare, but your degree of irrationality has led you above and beyond any place I could ever take you. You see *lies in truth*! As impressive a feat of absurdity as I've ever seen. Forget e pluribus unum. Yours should be a motto of a different sort. Like old Aesop's fox to the frog: medice, cura te ipsum. Physician, heal thyself!"

The old man reeled and laughed heartily, the pages of his face splitting from ear to ear in a grotesque, crinkly grin. The steely blade of his teared *couteau de chasse*, now nothing more than a paper cutout folded in half, tore beneath his leg as he rolled back in his seat. Composing himself, he began refilling his papier-mâché pipe with shreds of brown kraft paper, then reached for a match from the box on the table. Striking the flame, he paused to consider the burning stick grasped between his flimsy, onion-skinned fingers, then wisely dropped it in his empty wineglass.

"Perhaps a final measure of merlot instead," he said. "I believe I spied a bottle of '52 behind the bar earlier. Would you be so kind?"

I left the table to retrieve the wine, hopeful that obliging his whim would prolong his stay.

"A bottle of the Bordeaux '52," I said to the bartender.

"That some kind of a joke?" he replied, unamused.

"I'm sorry?"

"Got a '19 house white and a couple of bottles of Shiraz. Maybe a pinot noir, I'd have to go downstairs to check. Other than that, it's what I got out here," he said, gesturing to the rows of bottles lined up behind the bar.

Cheap swill, the lot of it. Disappointed, I had just turned to go back to our table when I suddenly felt a strange feeling rising up from within give me pause. Call it an uncharacteristic sensation of flourishing grandiosity. A confidence I'd hitherto not felt. My shoulders squared and my chest filled with soldierly swell. My chin, of its own accord, haughtily thrust itself forward like a bayonet in the barkeep's face as I ordered with bravado:

"Then a bottle of your finest cabernet sauvignon, and make haste, my fine fellow," I said, my voice assuming a nasally exuberance as I wrapped my knuckles smartly on the sticky bar top. "And allow me to dispense a tidbit of wisdom. You'd best not forget Rabelais's discourse on the subject of wine. Chase the mad dog so that he never bites you, eh? If you drink *before* the thirst, it will never come to you. Now, then, what does this establishment offer a road-weary traveler to complement his draught? Hopefully no mere provender. Perhaps a plate of gouda with andouille?"

The bartender remained unmoved. The devastatingly unimpressed look on his face sucked the wind from my bombastic sails and left me hopelessly adrift in a sea of awkwardness. The silence was painful, punctuated only by the honk of a car horn somewhere up the street.

My shoulders sunk as I drew my hand back from the bar.

"Another Stella," I said meekly, my voice returned to its usual unassuming tenor. By way of apology, I left a ten and slunk back to my table with my beer, there to find nothing waiting for me but a damp coaster and used, dog-eared copy of *Tristram Shandy*. No glasses of claret, no unfinished plate of oily kippers, no loose shreds of burley tobacco dotting the floor. Just an empty chair.

I took up my book and left.

EPILOGUE

"So, then, your expedition proved a fruitful one, Baron. We've had the pleasure of perusing some of your reports. These little—what do they call them, *tweets, bleats?*—are of singular amusement. Our best minds will be taking a closer look at your notes very soon. I've no doubt your observations will serve as the source of many more volumes to come."

"I am humbled by Your Grace's optimism. I viewed my task as nothing less than my duty and honor to undertake in the hope some good would come out of it for the benefit of you and your people. I understand work has already begun on a new wing of the Munchausen Athenaeum in my absence."

"Yes, to house a research facility dedicated to studying the ills of the dialectic in American society so as to identify the seeds of it in our own before they can be allowed to germinate. We cannot in all good conscience permit such rationality to pervade here as it has down there. It could be devastating to our own civilization."

"I could not agree more with Your Lunarship's assessment. With your permission, I should like to volunteer my services in any way I can. Perhaps Your Grace would see it wisest to install Munchausen in an administrative role in this research?"

"We are humbled by your sacrifice, Baron. The survival of lunar society may very well depend on your diligent perspicacity. Mercifully, irrationality is innate in our culture, so there is little to fear in the masses suddenly developing a taste for American-style truths. We Lunarians, at least, still regard things with an open mind. But still, after reading your assessment, our hearts go out to them in their time of need. Tell us, are the Americans as doomed as you say? Is there really no hope for them?"

"Well, I suppose that would really depend. Tell me, Your Highness, how familiar are you with Laplace's ninth principle?"